MESSENGER OF THE REAPER

PART 2

REVENGE

JIMMY AND ANGELYN STRALEY

This book is dedicated to my wife and editor Angelyn,
and all my friends that gave me the ideal of what
they thought would make this a great story.

CHAPTER 1

Driving down the road to Baton Rouge to do my first assignment for my new job, I kept thinking about my friend James that had just passed away not long ago. I had to do this job without any mistakes. I had my brother in law, Timothy, watching over me and reporting to my new boss. His evaluation of my potential ability to accurately perform the tasks necessary to professionally perform my new job. Although at this time, the only thing he was evaluating, were the inside of his eyelids while lying in the back seat. I wasn't making much on this job, but at least I had a job, and it involved getting vengeance on those that had done me and my family wrong. Well, everyone has to start at the bottom whenever they start a new job. It won't take me long to move up. As I crossed the Louisiana border, I began to look for a place to get gas and breakfast, none of us ran on air. As I pulled up to the pump and shut down the engine Tim raised up with a sleepy look on his face, and looked around asking where we were. Telling him that we were in Louisiana and that I was hungry, the car was thirsty, and I needed to stretch my legs, he just nodded his head. Getting out of the car, and stumbling a little bit, Tim stretched and yawned, waking up.

"Sounds like a good idea to me, I could use some breakfast myself." Tim said.

"It's your turn to drive after breakfast, I have been driving all night and I need to get some rest," I told him.

After the car was filled, we went inside and sat down at a table and waited for the waitress to come take our order. When she got there, she asked us if we would like some coffee, and we both nodded our heads in agreement and then took the menus that she had in her hand for us. Looking over the menu we had already chosen what we wanted by the time she returned with our coffee. Taking out her pad she jotted down our orders and left. As we waited for our food to arrive, we started discussing the plans for the job that had been assigned to us.

"Paul, I am sorry about this being a low paying job, but Rudy told me that we first have to test you and see what you know. We have had other people that were supposed to be good and turned out to know nothing at all, and mess up on their first assignment." Tim said.

"I am not worried about the pay at this time as long as I can make a living. I am more interested in getting help finding the ones that are responsible for this mess and James' death." I told him.

"Well don't let that get in your way of doing your job. That could cause you to make a fatal mistake." Tim responded.

Looking Tim straight in the eyes and loosing all expression on my face I said to him in a stern voice, "I will do my job to the best of my ability in a professional manner. If anybody gets in my way, including you I will take them out as well, is that understood?"

Tim's face turned a little pale, and looking down he answered, "Yes I fully understand, but where did you go? While you were just talking I could swear that I saw death there in your face. That look actually scared me a little and sent goose bumps down my spine."

"He just might have been, no one knows what I learned when James and I were together, but me. Some of the stuff I learned from him would turn your hair white. I intend to use everything that I know to get any job that I have done right. The worst part of it all is that we are in the place where it all started for James, and there were a lot of secrets that he never told me. I found out a lot of his secrets for myself the hard way, and there is no way I can return from where I am now." I told Tim with a bit of regret and satisfaction at the same time in my voice.

"Will you try and explain some of the secrets to me so that maybe I can understand what you are going through?" Tim asked.

"No, Sorry I won't even tell Sara about most of it! I don't think she could handle it without having a mental break down. As far as you are concerned, well, after I have proven myself and gotten to those responsible, we will no longer be together. Then it will just be me and all my burdens together for all of eternity as far as I know." I answered Tim.

Finishing up breakfast, we got ready to continue our trip, requested some coffee to go, and I told Tim to make sure that he woke me up when we got near our destination. I wanted to see how the town was laid out so I could make plans on how to leave in a hurry if necessary. Tim told me that it wasn't going to be a problem. Pulling out of the drive I turned on the radio and found a station that was playing classical rock, and then leaned my head over on the door, closed my eyes and went to sleep knowing that my friend was watching over me. When I opened my eyes I noticed a sign that said that we were only five miles from our destination. Sitting up I told Tim that we needed to stop somewhere when we got into town, since that coffee was going right through me. Nodding his head he started looking for a gas station or some place that had a restroom to pull over at. It wasn't until we passed the city limit sign that we noticed a small mom and pop gas station to pull in to. After we had finished our business at the gas station and gotten a drink to go, we were back on the road again. I asked Tim where the files were on the guy we were hired to take out, so I could refresh my mind on where and what he might be doing. Turning around Tim reached into the back seat grabbed his little case and pulled out the file. Opening it up, Tim began thumbing through it and asked me what it was that I wanted to know.

"Well this is Friday morning, so I know he is probably at work, where does he normally go Friday nights?" I asked Tim.

"Let me look here, it says that he normally goes to a bar out on the edge of town." Tim answered giving me the address to where it was located. Telling Tim to punch the address into the GPS system I had, we headed towards the bar. When Tim noticed that I was directing him towards the bar, he looked over at me and commented "The bar is not open right now. Why arc we going there right now?"

"I want to see where this place is located and what it looks like around it. Since the place is closed, I can see what it looks like, and make plans according to the area there." I answered Tim. Nodding at me Tim gave me the thumbs up as we continued to drive towards the bar. After we reached our destination we got out and I started to look around accessing the layout so I could come up with a plan. The first thing I noticed was that the place was way out in the middle of nowhere and not far away there was stream that was part of the swamp, maybe that's why they called this place The Swamp Inn. Walking down to the waters edge I noticed a place on the ground that looked like some kind of animal lived there. Considering the area where I was, my first thought was, it must be an alligator. Perfect. I just might be able to use that in my favor, now I just had to figure out how. Continuing to inspect the grounds and everything else there, I couldn't find much else that would be of any help. Walking over to Tim I told him that it was time to go and that we also needed to stop by a store somewhere to get something. Not saying anything, Tim looked at me then just turned around and headed back to the car with a strange look on his face. As we left I noticed that Tim kept looking straight ahead or out the side window of the car as if he was avoiding looking at me. Driving down the road we found a multi department store that sold more than groceries. Pulling into an available parking space, I parked and we both got out, going inside. He was curious as to what I needed at the store to do the job. Walking in I headed to the hardware section to find some clothes line rope, then I head to the food side to find me a nice plump chicken. Tim was dumbfounded at the choice of items that I had picked out to use in this job, but simply observed, and shook his head from side to side.

Getting back out to the car Tim asked me, "What is the stuff you just bought for?"

"I don't know, something just told me I needed to get this stuff while I was out there at the bar. Lately I have been having a lot of thoughts to do things that I don't know where they come from. All I know is that I always end up using it, or do whatever it is that popped into my head," I answered Tim as I drove out on to the road. Now all we had to do was find something to occupy our time until the bar opened and our mark showed up. Thinking for a bit, I decided we could go look around town and just do some sight seeing until it was time to go.

Time seemed to fly as we went from store to store, just looking around and enjoying ourselves. Noticing the sun was going down I looked at my watch and told Tim that it was time to get back over to the bar and find our mark. We had our job cut out for us since all we had was a name and no picture, to indicate who to look for in that place. The best thing describing him that we had was that he was a rowdy loudmouth that couldn't hold his liquor very well, and that he had a bad reputation.

Pulling into the driveway at the bar I turned to Tim telling him, "We might be here for a while so watch what and how much you drink; you won't be of any use to me if you're drunk while we are working. Here is what we are going to do, we go in and order a drink and find a place to sit and watch the crowd and see who has got the biggest mouth. Then we will ask a few questions as to who the loudmouth is, most of them in there should know. After that I will go outside and get set up and I will need about ten minutes to get things ready. Then, you will get his attention and get him to go outside to the back of the lot, but make sure you don't follow him. I will take care of the rest when he gets back there, and after he's out, you get over to the car and start it up so we can leave from here right away. Now I hope that you understand all that because I am not going to repeat it," I told him.

"I understand all of that but would you quit doing that thing with your face every time you talk about the job." Tim asked.

"Doing what? I am not doing anything with my face." I told Tim.

"Yes you are, every time that you start to speak of a job it looks like you have another face, and a whole other attitude. It is like death is trying to take over and looking me right in the face, it's creepy." Tim said.

"Well I am not aware of anything like that but I will try to control it for you." I told Tim. Then I told Tim to go on into the bar, find us a table where we could see everything going on while I went around back to check on something. Just nodding and getting out of the car, Tim headed into the bar and I went around back to see if the gator nest was occupied or not. Reaching the back of the lot I looked through the brush and thicket, and there it was. A nice large gator about ten feet in length. Perfect I thought. Not wanting to disturb it I slowly backed away and went in to join Tim inside the bar. Walking in I noticed a live band playing onstage, and several tables positioned around the dance floor in the middle of the bar. It took me a few minutes to adjust my eyes to the low lighting and spot Tim sitting off at a table in a far back corner where we could look over the whole place. I couldn't have picked a better place myself even if had wanted to. Making my way over to Tim I sat down at the table he had chosen with my back to the wall so that I had a good view of the scenery inside. I had only been sitting there for a few minutes when a nice looking young lady came up to us asking what we would have. Ordering us both a beer she left and I began to scan the room looking for the one that was causing the most ruckus in here. Since the night was still young everyone seemed to be behaving themselves right now, but give it a while, and let them get a few beers down, and that would change. Conveniently though, this wasn't too bad of a place to wait around at, there were plenty of pretty women to look at and the band wasn't that bad. They were playing a good mix of country and western along with some old classic rock and the choice made a very good sound together.

For the next couple of hours Tim and I just sat there enjoying ourselves watching for a loudmouth and dancing with some of the women so we could talk to them and see if they could give us a clue to what this person looked like that we were looking for. The biggest clue that I kept getting was about this guy who thought he was so big and bad that he would actually go outside to take a wiz on Old Mike out back. Asking who Old Mike was, I was told that he was the gator that had lived behind the bar for years now. When I heard this I thought to myself, I may not need that chicken I bought after all. While I was dancing with a nice looking older lady I noticed this burly looking man was starting to act as if he was the biggest, meanest one in the place. He was wearing blue jeans with tears in both knees, and a checkered long sleeved shirt, with the sleeves rolled halfway up, to display his muscular arms. His face was unshaven, displaying a beard, long and shaggy looking, the same color as his hair, a dark reddish brown. Stopping in the middle of the dance I looked over at him trying to decide if he was the one we were after here. The woman looked over in the direction that I was staring, and told me that was Donald Mitch, and to ignore him, he was always like that when he drank, and in a little bit he would try to show off by going out and taking a wiz on Old Mike. Pretending to ignore him, I finished the dance, and then returned to my table with Tim. Telling Tim that I had found our man, I pointed Donald out, and then told him that the lady that had been dancing with me had identified him for me.

"We have a little change in plans, I have been told that he has a dangerous habit, so when he walks out of the back door, I just need you to go to the car and get ready to go." I told Tim.

Sitting there, I watched as Donald slammed down three more beers, so I figured that it was about time for him to have to relieve himself, and the fact that he was feeling bullet proof, I made my way out of the bar, heading towards the car. Once I got there, I opened the trunk and removed the knife that my friend James had loaned me a while back, and I never got to return. I really liked it; it had a long stiff blade with brass knuckles built on the handle. Placing it on my side, I made my way around to the back of the bar to wait on Donald to come out to perform his ritual on Old Mike.

Not having to wait very long, I could hear him heading my way, hollering at the gator about how much better he was than him. Checking to see which way he was coming, I positioned myself in front of a car that was parked there, so that he could not see me, and then waited for him to stumble by with his drunken ass past me. In that moment, I had a feeling come over me, like I was there and knew what was going on, but I was no longer in control of what I was doing. He made his way to the front of one of the cars I was crouched down behind, then leaned back and started undoing his zipper. Stumbling towards Old Mike he mumbled something about how one day he is going to make him into a suitcase or something like that. Just as he started to let loose I sprung up behind him placing one foot in front of his, and then I shoved him hard. He stumbled forward a couple of steps, and then fell flat on his face about two inches in front of Old Mike. Lunging forward, Old Mike took charge, opening his giant mouth, and then clamping down on Donald's head. You could hear his muffled screams from inside the gators mouth as Old Mike began to thrash him from side to side, while Donald was attempting to beat at the gators head. After a few moments Old Mike quit shaking Donald and bit down, and there was an amazingly loud snap as all of Donald's limbs twitched at the same time. Looking down at the mess of blood and urine all over the place I laughed as the gator chewed and swallowed the part he had bitten off. I think he must have shit on himself as well, judging by the smell, and I think Old Mike smelled it too, because he slid back off into the murky waters of the swamp, leaving the rest of Donald's torn carcass where it laid, and was gone. As the gator emerged back into the water, that feeling that had come over me at the beginning of all this was gone.

Getting a cold chill, I looked up and noticed my friend James, the Reaper, standing there giving me a thumbs up signal. Smiling back at him I knew what I had to do next, so I turned around and headed towards the bar. Walking around to the front, I stuck my head in the door and yelled out above the music, "Hey there is some fool out back wrestling a gator and I think he is loosing!"

As soon as I said that, everyone stopped what they were doing and headed towards the back door. The barkeep just said "I don't know how many times I told that dumbass S.O.B. to leave that damn gator alone!" and headed towards the back door. Since everyone was headed out the back I went out the front and got in the car with Tim, and we left unnoticed and in a leisurely manner.

"Are we headed back home now?" Tim asked.

"No, not tonight, we can just get a room and head back in the morning. "All the evidence that they can find points to a drunken dumbass fighting with a gator and loosing." I said.

"How did you manage that?" Tim asked.

Not really knowing for sure how to answer that question, because I didn't really have the knowledge as to how I was doing it myself, I hesitated and then responded "I let him do it to himself with a little extra help he didn't expect." I said, smiling sadistically.

Debating about whether or not to try and explain to Tim what was going on, I reached over to turn the heater on and caught a glimpse of James in the rear view mirror, sitting in the back seat shaking his head no, and then he vanished. Taking that as a sign I should keep this little secret to myself, I said nothing and just sat back and enjoyed the ride.

After leaving Baton Rouge, we stopped at the first cheap motel that we could find to settle down for the rest of the night. Getting signed in, we proceeded to our room for a hot shower and some well deserved rest. Once in the room Tim said, "I need you to explain to me how you took care of Donald, so that I can explain to Rudy what happened when I call him tomorrow."

Motioning Tim to sit down on the corner of his bed, I carefully went over the events that led up to Donald's demise, leaving out certain things that he did not need to know. After I had finished, I went to take a hot shower, wishing that I had someone I could talk to, and help to explain all these strange things going on with me now. But for now, all I could do was just carry on and act like nothing was going on but work as usual. By the time I got out of the shower, Tim had already fallen asleep, but I was wide awake so I decided to get dressed and take a walk around. Stepping outside, I took a deep breath and just started walking, enjoying the cool night air and the smell of the trees and crops that were familiar to this area. Having walked only a couple of blocks, I passed an old woman that had matted hair and was bent over, with a tattered old shawl draped over her head.

As I walked past her she spoke, saying "I see you and your friend are still together. Just be patient, and all will be explained in time."

Then I heard her laughing in a familiar cackling voice. Turning around I looked back where she was crouched and I couldn't see her, she was gone! Was she the same old witch that James had told me about when we were together, and where did she come from, but most importantly where did she go? That was it, I was returning to the room and going to bed, I'd seen enough strange occurrences for one night.

Waking up the next morning, Tim had already gotten up and was just stepping out of the shower. After my morning trip to the bathroom, I turned on the television looking for the news. It took flipping through several channels before I could find any news reports. Sitting down on the corner of the bed Tim and I both listened intently for any mention about last night. After about ten minutes it was finally mentioned on the news, a story about a local idiot that got killed playing with the towns' infamous alligator, Old Mike. Going to a live feed it showed the scene where Donald's remains were, and the mess left behind on the ground. They even went into details about how people were telling them that Donald had a habit of tormenting the gator that lived there. After reporting the story they gave out a public service announcement about how nobody should mess with alligators, and if they felt threatened to call the authorities for help.

"I thought you were kidding last night when you told me how you did that, but it looks like you were telling the truth. I never would have thought of something like that, using nature to help you carry out your job and letting mother nature get all the blame. Brilliant!" Tim exclaimed.

"Its easy if you just look around at what's there and think about it logically. There is always something lying around that you can use to your advantage if you know how to look." I said.

Then I smiled at him, knowing that I didn't have any clue as to what I was going to do when I got there or how I was going to do it. If it were not for the strange feelings of being possessed that I had been getting, that gave me the clues that I needed, or I wouldn't have known what to do. I wasn't about to try and explain to him how I was getting this knowledge since I didn't even know myself.

Grabbing his phone, Tim called Rudy to tell him that the job was done in a flawless manner, and how I had made it look like an accident. As he was explaining it all to Rudy, he stepped outside the door, shutting it behind him as he exited. I began to make sure everything was packed and ready to go, so that when he came back in we would be ready to leave.

Walking back in Tim said, "Rudy told me to tell you congrats and good thinking using nature to cover the hit, he would have never thought of that. Your money will be in the bank tonight. Now that's taken care of, let's go and get some breakfast, I'm hungry. I also have some news to tell you, but it can wait. Some of it is good, and some is bad."

CHAPTER 2

Grabbing our bags, I sent Tim to return the room key, while I put all of our things in the car. By the time he got back, I had everything ready to go. Leaving out, all I could think about was how nice it would be to get back home, away from all of this side of the road food, that didn't taste as good as home. Finding a fairly nice looking little place we pulled in and found a spot around the back to park. As we made our way around to the front, Tim appeared to be in a real happy mood, smiling and waving at everyone with a slight dance in his step. Once inside, we selected a table near the back and took a seat, ordering breakfast and coffee. Once the waitress had brought the coffee, I fixed it to my liking and after tasting it, I was glad that I had not left the spoon in it too long. As strong as it was, the spoon might have melted just sitting in there, I thought to myself. I wouldn't need more than two cups of this to keep me going all day. As our food arrived, I remembered that Tim had said he had some news to tell me and that we would discuss it over breakfast.

Looking over at Tim I said, "You said you had some news to tell me and I am anxious to hear what you have to say."

Swallowing the food in his mouth Tim asked, "Do you want the good news or the bad news first?"

"Well I would suggest that you start somewhere and get it over with, I don't like playing games." I said sternly.

"Well I'm sure you remember the list that you gave Rudy of the people that you are looking for. One of them has showed up, a Mr. Robert Downhill. That's the good news that I have for you, now for the bad news. He is in police custody and is being transported back to Dallas Tuesday morning, since he agreed to talk. If he decides to talk, then its game over for all of them, us included. We won't be able to do anything while they are locked up." Tim informed me.

"No, he won't tell them everything, and I can assure you it won't be over. We are going to have to break him out, and take care of things ourselves in order for this nightmare that is tormenting my family to be over with. Did he say what time he would be in Dallas Tuesday morning?" I asked Tim.

"All I know is that he said he would be taken in front of the judge at ten o'clock Tuesday morning." Tim said.

"Good, I know what judge he will be seeing; all I have to do now is devise a plan to get him away from the cops that will be escorting him to the courtroom to testify. Are you in, or are you going to chicken out on this one?" I asked Tim.

"I don't know, it sounds awfully risky. Are you sure that you can come up with a plan that won't get us both behind bars?" Tim asked.

"Yeah I'm sure I can do that, I will just have to think for a bit and go look around. After we finish eating, we are heading to Dallas so that I can see what we are up against, and what is going to have to be done." I informed Tim.

"I will call and make a reservation at a motel since your place got taken out and is no longer available." Tim said.

"No, there is no sense in that I have a place that we can stay at while we are there, and it won't cost us anything." I told Tim.

Finishing up our meal and taking care of the tab, we made our way back to the car, and then headed off to Dallas. As I was driving, I had a million scenarios playing out in my head, on how we were going to get Robert, and what I was going to do to him once we had him. I wanted him to hurt and suffer a lot before he died, so that he could think about what he had agreed upon when he became a threat to my family. The miles seemed to pass slowly as we rolled down the highway. I guess it was because of the anticipation of what was about to happen.

Once we arrived in Dallas, I drove downtown to the courthouse and parked, so that I could take a walk around and see what we were up against to break Robert out. Since he was not out on bond he wouldn't be coming in the front, so there had to be another entrance for prisoners to be taken in at. Slowly easing around the building I looked at everything, around and on the building, memorizing the entire layout, so that I could figure out what had to be done next. Getting around to the back I found the prisoner entrance with two cameras pointing towards the door so that what ever went on there could be recorded. After seeing that, I looked across the street, and all over the surrounding buildings to see if there were any more cameras located anywhere near that could see this part of the building. Once I had the entire building committed to memory, I went across the street to see if there was a place that I could hide and have an advantage point. After checking out about ten different places that I had found, I added them to the layout of the building in my head. Now it was time to go to my place where I could mull over all of this new information, and come up with the perfect plan to get this done without getting caught. Motioning to Tim we went back to my car, and then we were on our way to get some rest and relax a bit, and discuss what we were going to do come Tuesday.

When I turned into the parking garage where we were going to stay, Tim's eyes got wide as he exclaimed, "This is where we are going to stay while we are here?"

"Yeah I own a place here." I told him.

With a surprised look on his face, he turned toward me saying, "Damn I thought you and Sara were having a hard time. All I've heard was how she was having to work too because you were not making enough, or was this another present from the Ghost, like that place out in West Texas?" Tim asked.

"That doesn't matter right this minute, all I will say is that Sara and I are doing good now, and have very little to worry about. Maybe someday I will be able to explain it all to you, but for right now all we need to be worrying about is the job at hand, and that means getting this contract off me and my family's head." I told Tim.

Nodding his head he replied, "True, and I fully understand what you mean there."

Parking the car, we got out, and grabbed our bags, and the two special cases in the trunk, and then we headed up to the condo. On the ride up in the elevator, Tim asked, "What is so special about those two cases you always carry around with you, I've never even seen you open them?"

"Don't worry about what's in them, just know that when the time comes, you will find out. They might even save your life." I replied.

Tim just nodded. As the elevator doors opened on our floor, we stepped out, and I unlocked the doors to my condo. Tim was astonished as he looked around at all the lavish furniture and expensive paintings on the wall. The carpet was a dark red that matched the color of the living room furnishings. The walls were painted in a royal blue, which also went with the living room decor. His eyes widened as they came to rest on a giant 60 inch flat screen TV in the far corner of the room.

Looking back at me Tim said, "There is a fortune in this room alone!"

I simply responded, "Yeah," Then I showed him where he would be sleeping, and where to put his things. I then turned and headed into the master bedroom to put my things away. Afterwards I headed back towards the kitchen, pen and pad in hand, I sat down to begin drawing out a map of everything I had memorized, and devising a master plan of how we were going to break Mr. Downhill out of protective custody.

I drew a diagram of the building and surrounding area from memory with cameras marked as an x. Then I started to study the diagram, trying to decide which would be the best approach to come from. After a couple of hours, I had a plan fabricated in my head, but I would need to go back over it, and study the layout with the plan that I had formed. But by this time, it had gotten late, and I needed to get some rest. We still had two days before Mr. Downhill was scheduled to arrive. Picking up my things and putting them away for the night, I passed through the den, advising Tim not to stay up too late, we had some work to do in the morning. I headed for the master bedroom, and decided a quick shower sounded good. After I took care of all my shower needs and hygiene routines for the night, I made a quick call to Sara, to let her know what was going on, and to check on the kids. After I hung up, I laid down, my head buzzing with different scenarios and outcomes of the decisions I had made tonight while planning.

The next morning, I wasn't very sure of the decisions I had made, but I was still going to go back out and check everything over one last time. Going into the kitchen I put on a pot of coffee, and then yelled down the hallway at Tim, that it was time to get up. Stumbling into the kitchen, Tim grabbed a cup, and poured himself some coffee, and then he sat down at the table. As he started to drink his coffee, he noticed all the drawings and plans laid out on the table, and his eyes got wide. "Damn, you are really going to break him out, I thought you were only joking about that!" Tim declared in an excited and surprised tone.

"I don't play around when it comes to doing my job." I told him in a stern voice.

Walking over to him and looking him straight in the eyes I added in an even sterner voice, "You do know it's already too late for you to back out now, you already know too much. If you even try, I will have to kill you myself."

I could see Tim's face go pale as he returned my stare. It was as if he had seen something there that had frightened him. Staring back at me, he only nodded his head in agreement. Knowing that I had totally frightened him, I brought our attention back to the job at hand. Pointing back to the plans that I had laid out on the table I started to go over with him what I had thought what would be the best way to get the job done. I also told him that we needed to go back over and spend some time studying the layout; if we couldn't find a way to do this without getting caught, then we wouldn't do it at all. A relieved look came over his face as I made the last statement.

As Tim looked over the plans he said, "These plans you drew up are very detailed, it as if I am looking at a surveyors map. I don't know how you can remember so many details and then draw them down like a map without taking pictures."

"Just something that I was taught to do; if you are finished we need to get going. We have a lot a lot of work to get done." I told Tim.

Nodding his head he gulped down the last bit of coffee he had, and started putting on his shoes. Getting up from the table I joined him by the door so that we could leave and head for downtown.

The ride to the courthouse was an uneventful one, no one spoke a word. It was a quiet ride, and we relaxed the whole way. Once we reached our destination I found a parking place, and then informed Tim that I would be at the park across from the courthouse where I could observe the activities there. Tim decided to go for a stroll around town to see what he could find, and that was fine with me. It just meant that I didn't have to put up with his never ending questions. After sitting there for about two hours I finally got to see what I really needed to know. A cop car pulled up with a prisoner, and after coming to a stop, the officer got out and waved a sign at a hidden camera above the door then stood back and waited for about thirty seconds. A detective opened the door, and stepped out, taking charge of the prisoner. Picking up my binoculars I searched for the camera at the place where the cop waved the sign but, all I could see was a hole in the wall. There had to be a camera there but I couldn't see it, so there was no way to take it out without being seen doing so. All my plans were now ruined, so I had to come up with another way to do this. Looking around I noticed Tim was heading back from his excursion around town. When he got to where I was waiting, I handed him the car keys and told him to go get the car. When he pulled around to where I was, I would be ready to go. I only had a few more things to look at before he got back with the car. Tomorrow was Monday, so I needed to come by and see how busy this place got, before I could make any final plans to make sure that Mr. Downhill didn't get the chance to run his mouth, and mess up all of my plans. It took about five minutes before I noticed Tim pulling up to the turn lane by the park. Good I thought, I am ready to get out of this place for now.

Tim pulled up to the curb, and as I got in and shut the door he asked in a playful tone, "Where to now Boss?"

With a slight grin on my face because he sounded like an old movie actor, I told him "If you are ready for lunch I know a little café close by here. It's where James and I first met, and they have really good food."

I could see a slight grin form on his face as he answered with "That sounds good as long as James isn't there with us. I never got to meet James, but lately I could swear that you are not yourself, like a totally different person, and all I know is who ever it is, it's not you, and that person scares the shit out of me." Tim said.

"Well I can't promise anything that I don't have control over, but I will try my best to make sure that James doesn't show up." I said.

I tried to act like I didn't know what he was talking about, but the truth be known, I had been having some strange feelings that I couldn't explain myself. But I sure wasn't going to tell anyone about them and risk being locked up in a loony bin, and loose my chance at getting this bounty off my family's head. Mr. Downhill was just a small fish in the pond, but it would get some attention where it mattered.

After giving Tim directions to where we were going he slowly proceeded to the café. Finding a parking place Tim pulled in, and we headed inside so we could get us some lunch. As we entered the café, I saw a familiar face walking towards us. It was Alice. The same waitress that had taken care of me and my friend the last time I was here. Smiling at her I pointed towards the back of the café, and she nodded, motioning us to follow her.

Sitting us at a table Alice asked "Business or pleasure, and should I expect anyone else to arrive? Are you two having coffee or something else to drink today and do you need a menu?"

Looking over at Tim I asked "what will you have, sweet tea, a cola, or do you want something else?"

Thinking for a moment Tim replied "Sweet tea and a menu, I'm hungry." Alice then looked over at me and I nodded my head while giving her a thumbs up, indicating I would have the same. Turning away she left to get our tea and menus.

When Alice returned with our drinks and menus she looked at me and asked, "Where are your other two friends at today?" Not looking up at her I informed her that they had passed away during that incident at Kill Devil Hills in Virginia. With sorrow in her voice she said "So sorry to hear that, but wasn't that a shame that so many people lost their lives because of that underground coal fire? It all happened so suddenly." Nodding my head while still looking down, I agreed even though I knew the truth about what happened.

She agreed to give them a few minutes to go over their menus and decide what they were going to order, and then she would return. While looking at the menu, Tim brought up the statement the waitress had mentioned about three people having been there before.

"I know about James, but who else was here with you guys?" Tim asked curiously.

"That was when Michael introduced me to James," I replied.

Tim simply grunted in response. A few minutes later, Alice returned to take our order. After getting everything written down, she left to turn in our order. After she was gone, Tim began to ask me if I had learned everything I needed to learn today.

"Yes I did, but I'm not very happy about it." I responded.

"What do you mean?" Tim asked.

"Well, what I am saying is, we cannot do the job." I informed him.

"Does that mean we are going back to Texas tomorrow?" Tim asked.

"No, Raul said that he has something he wanted you to do Tuesday, since you're here, but we will leave as soon as he is done with you." I told him, hoping that I wasn't giving anything away in the tone of my voice.

I had to admit to myself that this job couldn't be done as a team, but I was still planning on taking care of business alone. I just needed to get a hold of Raul now, and arrange for him to keep Tim busy Tuesday morning. Problem solved. I hoped.

Alice appeared with our lunch, so conversation was placed on hold while we ate. As she placed it on the table, we began to devour the meal that was placed before us. After I finished my meal, I excused myself to go to the restroom. Once I was out of earshot of Tim, I called Raul. I then began to make arrangements for Tuesday. Raul was in agreement, he simply warned me to be careful. With that taken care of, I returned to the table, and by then Tim had finished. I asked Alice for two teas to go, and the check, then made my way to the front to pay, leaving a generous tip.

The next day and a half was going to be long, and I could not reveal any plans I was making to Tim, for fear of him trying to get involved. I turned my attention to what we could do to occupy our time. I was actually multitasking, by secretly continuing to plan out what had to be done to complete the job ahead in my mind. Time appeared to fly by for Tim, but for me, time seemed to drag on. I guess when you are the only one aware of everything going on, time seems to play with your mind. Ignorance is bliss. I now understand a whole lot better what James went through.

As Monday night finally rolled around I sighed, thinking to myself, tomorrow is the big day. As I lay down to rest, I caught a glimpse of James standing at the foot of my bed. He turned towards me and informed me, "I will be with you tomorrow, to help you get through this, the best way I know how," and then he vanished. "Great", I thought to myself, how can the reaper, who is basically a ghost, do anything to help me with my job? With that thought in my head I turned over and went to sleep.

As I awoke to the alarm, I had butterflies in my stomach, yet felt like I had ice running through my veins. What an interesting combination of feelings, I thought to myself. Getting up, I put some coffee on, and then returned to my room to get dressed. After getting ready, I checked on the coffee, and seeing that it was good, I poured two cups then went to get Tim up, since Raul would be there soon to get him. Letting Tim know that there was a cup of coffee waiting on him in the kitchen, and that he needed to put a move on, so he could pack all of his things and get them ready to load in the car. I informed him that he would he helping Raul at his shop today, and that he will call me and let me know when they are done for the day, so I could come and pick him up, and from there we would continue on to west Texas.

Between sips of coffee Tim asked "Do I need to go ahead and load my stuff in the car before I leave?"

"No, just put them by the door and I will get them when I load my stuff later." I answered him. Finishing off his coffee Tim went and packed all his things and placed them where he was told. After a few minutes we heard a knock at the door. Looking through the peep hole I verified that it was Raul. Hollering at Tim, that his ride was here, I told him it was time for him to go.

As Tim was heading out the door he turned around looked at me and said "I know it must be hard on you knowing that we are not able to do this job, but cheer up, things will get better." Nodding my head I waved at him, not wanting him to know that the job was still going to be done, just not with him included.

Giving them time to leave I went into my bedroom and opened up the case that held my laser rifle that I invented. Looking it over I made sure that it was in good working condition, since it was the only solution I had to get this job taken care of. After I was satisfied, I repacked it and took it out to the car, then headed out the door, to get the job taken care of.

Finding a place close by the park across from where Mr. Downhill would arrive, I grabbed the case with the rifle in it, and went to find me a good place to hide in the bushes where I could see the entrance and remain unseen. I looked at my watch and noticed that I had about an hour before he was scheduled to arrive. It was going to be a long wait I thought to myself. There was not much pedestrian traffic so that made it a lot easier for me, but I did have to get everything set up before it was time. By the time I had finished getting everything ready to go, I looked at my watch again and noticed that it was only about fifteen minutes before my mark was scheduled to arrive. Damn, time sure goes by quick sometimes! I didn't have to wait long before I noticed an unmarked police car coming down the street with his signal on indicating that he was about to turn into the Sally Port. Looking through my scope I could see Mr. Downhill in the back seat. My whole back suddenly stiffened, and I got an instant chill, like someone had put ice on it, and I knew that my friend James was there with me. I waited until they turned into the driveway between the two buildings, and had come to a complete stop, and then zeroed in on my marks head, and fired. I could see a hole form in his head through my scope before he fell sideways. Dead!!! He won't be talking any more. Packing my rifle up quickly, I got out of the bushes and headed for my car in a slow leisurely manner, like any other businessman on the street, carrying a briefcase. With a satisfied grin on my face, I got in and pulled away. My rifle had done its job, and made no noise while doing it. As I was driving away I noticed someone that looked familiar, standing by the driveway with an astonished look on his face, and when he turned around facing towards me, his face went pale. I didn't have time to stick around and find out who it was. There was already a lot of activity going on because their star witness had been killed while in protective custody. Going back to the condo, I packed all of mine and Tim's things into the car, and was off to Raul's to pick Tim up so we could go home, my job here was done for now.

CHAPTER 3

Arriving at Raul's, I noticed Tim was glued to his seat at the desk in the office listening to the radio. As I walked in, Tim turned towards me saying, "I thought you said the job was off."

I simply smiled at him and replied, "You're right. I said WE weren't going to be able to complete the job. I never said I couldn't do it myself."

Reaching over and turning a small TV on that was sitting on the desk, Tim turned on the midday news. As the reporter spoke, she described the scene where Robert Downhill was assassinated, and also the discovery of the usage of new superior weaponry, in which had only been seen once before. The details as to what government owned these weapons, and what their purpose was currently unknown. The FBI and the Department of Defense (DOD) were denying any knowledge of these weapons and are currently investigating the location of any said weapons, and who owned them. They were trying to determine whether or not these weapons were in our hands, or in enemy hands.

The police are also investigating a tip received from an eye witness who says he was walking down the street when he felt an intense heat wave in front of him for a brief second, and then the next he knew, the police were yelling about someone being dead. And then they showed a picture of the witness, and mentioned his name, Chris Gynas.

Seeing his face, I immediately knew who it was, and why his face seemed so familiar to me today. He was another one of the people on my list that had threatened my family, and needed to be dealt with. Well, it was too late now. He would be long gone by now. No matter, I WILL find him again.

Tim turned and looked at me with a question in his eyes and asked, "What are these advanced weapons that the reporter is talking about? Where did they come from, and who all knows about them?"

Looking him straight in the eye I replied, "The less you know, the better off you are. There are only two people that know about them, and one of them is dead. The only thing I will tell you is, that it's better for everyone involved that the government never find these weapons. And before you ask no, I will not show them to anyone, not even to you."

Tim then complains, "But we're supposed to be partners, and not have any secrets between us."

"Technically it's not really a secret, since you know about it. I am the professional and you are supposed to be the evaluator. There will always be things that I know, that you don't, that I can't share with you. Just like I expect you have things that you can't share with me. The most important thing is that we trust each other, and have each other's back, no matter what. Now, let's go home." I told him.

Nodding his head, Tim walked over and said his goodbyes and thanks to Raul, then went over to wait for me in the car. I thanked Raul for his help, and told him I would see him again later, and then left to join Tim.

On the way home I had Tim call Sara to let her know we were on our way there. I didn't like having her worry too much about me while I was out on a job. I could tell he wanted to tell his sister about our little adventure by the expression on his face, but luckily Rudy called Tim while he was on the phone with Sara. When he answered the call from Rudy his expression went from excited to all business in an instant. He didn't say much, mostly listening, and then told Rudy that he would call later with all the details that he could get, then hung up. Looking over at me Tim told me that he needed the details on how I had taken care of Robert Downhill so he could explain it to Rudy when he called him back later.

Reluctantly I began to explain about how I had noticed that there were some hidden cameras that we couldn't see, and why I knew that we would not be able to do the job together. I also explained about how it would be better if only one of us got caught instead of both. After I had finished with all the details I was willing to give, Tim once again asked about this strange gun that I had and how I was using it. Taking on my stern tone, I once again told him that there were some things that were better left alone and untold, just like he had information that he was not allowed to share with me as of yet. Nodding his head reluctantly in agreement, he then asked me why I had such an upset look on my face when this Chris Gynas was mentioned on the news.

Clearing my throat I began "Well Sara and I used to have a house here in Dallas until him and his accomplice planted a bomb in it. We were lucky that Sara and the kids were not home when it went off or they would have all been killed. They are both on my black list of revenge before this thing is all over. All I can do now is hope that his seeing what happened would smoke out the rest of them. Even if it doesn't, I will still track down each and every one of them and enact my rage upon them," I explained to Tim. As I was talking to Tim I could feel my face getting hot then cold as if something was happening, but I couldn't see my face since I didn't have anything to look at my reflection in. I wasn't sure what was going on but I could see Tim's facial expressions as he looked at me. I was beginning to realize that there were only two people that could explain what was going on and they were both supposedly dead. There was James, and I know he is dead to everyone but me, and then there was the old witch from Louisiana that seems to come and go as she pleases, and does what she wants, and I don't know how to get in touch with her. James doesn't talk so I am left with only one option; I need to find the old witch and ask her. We continued towards home, to take a short break between jobs, while I pondered my options before receiving another assignment.

As I turned on the road that led towards home, Tim's phone rang, and by the way he answered it, I could tell that it was Rudy, and by the way he was talking, I could tell we already had another job coming. I'd find out the details after we got settled down at the house. As we pulled into the drive, Sara came running outside to greet us. Before she got to the car, Tim informed me that indeed, Rudy had another job set up for us, and that we needed to be ready to leave within three days. I nodded in agreement, and Tim didn't say anything more about it. As we got out of the car Sara ran up and wrapped her arms around me, giving me a long kiss. Then she looked into my eyes, telling me how worried she had been, and how much she had missed me. She smiled at her brother, giving him a fond hug, and then we went inside.

As we entered the house we could smell the delicious aroma of dinner cooking. As Paul and I went to put our things away, Sara offered to carry my cases to the bedroom but I had to refuse since I didn't let anyone carry them but me. Looking at me somewhat confused, Sara told me "We need to talk. You don't act like the same person anymore." Nodding my head I simply replied "We'll talk later," then continued towards the bedroom carrying my cases with me so that I could hide them. She had never seen what I carried in those cases, nor did she have any idea how dangerous it could be to get caught with them in her possession. I was just now starting to realize just how dangerous it was to have them myself. Everyone wanted them. The police, other members of his own organization, hell even the government would kill to get their hands on this technology. The words that were spoken to me back when I was testing these weapons in the field for the first time by a dirty old hobo was starting to ring in my head, "Those weapons will mean the end of the world". The scary part is that my mentor and friend James, the one that still seems to be following me around, when he was still alive, agreed with the hobo. And now I am beginning to wonder if they weren't right. Now I could see a target on whoever has them in their possession, and I couldn't risk putting my family in anymore danger than they were already in.

After I had finished hiding away my weapons, I headed towards the kitchen and greeted my kids, getting showered with hugs and kisses from both of them. After hugging everyone, I decided to go take a shower and clean up before dinner. While I was in the shower, I got to thinking again about my weapons. I started wondering if after I got my family off the current hit list, if they wouldn't be replaced on another one because of them, or knowledge of them. I still need to catch up with the old witch so I can gain more knowledge of what's going on. I also recall that Tim said that we had another job in a few days, but I'm not sure where yet. Finishing my shower, I got out, and got dressed, then joined the rest of the family for dinner.

Setting down at the table, Sara brought out a nice meal of meatloaf, mashed potatoes, and green beans, along with some steaming rolls, and a large pitcher of iced tea. With heads bowed, Sara said grace, and then we began to serve and eat, while enjoying pleasant conversation with the children. After the children finished eating, they excused themselves, leaving the adults to discuss business.

Tim started the conversation mentioning that there was a job in Broken Bow, Oklahoma. Nodding my head in agreement, I told him that I would get the details from him later. We chatted for a while then I asked if he wouldn't mind giving me and my wife some time alone to talk. At that, Tim arose to go and play with the kids in the other room. After Tim left, Sara asked me what was going on, why I had been acting so differently lately. Looking her directly in the eyes, I told her that I wasn't really sure myself. "Tim has mentioned some strange things that he said he noticed me do as well, that I can't explain, and I don't understand. I'm still looking for an explanation, but I don't where to look for one yet."

"Well that answers that question," Sara said, "but I would still like to know what the deal is with those suitcases of yours."

"Well, concerning the projects I was working on a while back, those are the finished products. Fortunately they turned out much better than I ever expected them to. Unfortunately, they are so good, that everybody has a want for them. But they are original, and at the moment, they cannot be copied, and the only plans for them, are locked away in my head where I plan to keep them. One problem is however, whoever possesses them, becomes a target of many, including government officials. Have you heard about this high tech weaponry they've been talking about on the news?" Sara nodded in agreement. "That's what is in those cases. I can't share them with anyone because if they were to be mass produced, I have a feeling it would cause mass world destruction. Even if I destroyed them, there is still a danger that someone would discover what I've made, and that could still put you and the kids in danger. I am unable to decide what to do right now, I need to find someone James had told me about, so I can come up with a plan."

"Ok, let's go eat dessert, and we can talk more about this later," Sara said. She exited the room, heading towards the kitchen, preparing to place dessert on the table, while I went to collect Tim and the kids. She brought out a homemade apple pie, which had a smell that set the mouth to watering the instant she entered the room. We all sat down for dessert, and no one spoke a word, everyone simply enjoying the moment. Once we were all done, she cleared the table, while the kids prepared for bath time, and ultimately bedtime.

The time had come to continue my conversation with Tim about our upcoming job in Oklahoma. Tim placed his laptop on the table, and pulled up the file that had been sent by Rudy. As we reviewed the file, I noticed that our target was a little out of the ordinary. This target was an active duty narcotics police officer, who was accused of retaining a large portion of the drugs acquired on raids, and reselling them on the street for personal profit. The good thing is that the price for executing this job paid better. I guess this means I'm moving up the ladder. Higher profiles, higher pay. When I asked Tim how we caught this job, he told me it was because of my personal touch I used on the job I pulled solo in Dallas. When he said that, I simply smiled.

The target was an Italian playboy male in his mid-forties, notorious for juggling multiple women at once. Also known for using his badge to attract women, he was the perfect example of a worthless cop. He was 5'11", and attractive, with dark hair and eyes, and olive colored skin. He wouldn't be hard to track down. He was known on the street as the loaded Italian female magnet, driving fast cars, and always hanging out at bars and flashy hotels. He was known to all as Johnny Mancini. We would be leaving within a few days to rid the world of this trash.

We spent the next several hours going over his routine, becoming familiar with his beat, and schedule. We familiarized ourselves with the evidence that made him our target. Tomorrow I would devise a plan to use my 30.06 gun and a 30.06 accelerator bullet, with a silencer, so that there will be no rifling on the bullet that can be traced. If I can figure out how to accomplish this, I will it explain it all to Tim tomorrow. This should go off without a hitch. According to his files, he is already under investigation for multiple charges of fraud, theft, evidence tampering, unlawful use of force, multiple unlawful arrests, and so on. This looked like an easy target. But I would not know until I got there to see for myself what we were up against.

It was getting late, so we decided it was time to part company and get ready for bed. We had a lot of preparations and testing of weaponry before deciding what would be best in this case. Tomorrow would be a busy day, especially now that I was home, even if only for a few days, I had every intention of spending what time I could with my family as well. They deserved so much more. We put away our work, and I headed for bed, where my wife was waiting for me.

Lying down in bed I cuddled up next to my wife trying to forget about today, and get some wifely attention before some well needed sleep. As I lay there in bed, a million different scenarios and outcomes kept running through my mind. Even after falling asleep they continued coursing through my head taking over my dreams. Needless to say, I didn't get much rest that night. I could envision a lot of those things becoming reality and a lot of them I did not like the ending to. Oh well, I would have to deal with that stuff later if it came to it. For now, it was time for the kids to get up and get them ready for school, and for me to get my stuff ready to leave tomorrow. First thing I had to do was to round up the ammunition that I would need on my upcoming job, and make sure that it worked properly. After about two and a half hours in my work shop I had a hundred rounds for my rifle. Now it was time to see if it would work like I designed it to.

Grabbing my 30.06 rifle I headed outside to find a place to try out my newly made bullets. After finding a good clearing, I paced off a thousand yard range to shoot down. Placing my bore sighter in its place, I tuned my scope in for the long range shot that I was about to attempt. After making sure it was ready, I grabbed my target and started walking down range to place it where I needed it for my practice shot. As I made my way back to where I was going to be shooting from, I could see Tim walking towards me waving as he came. When he got to where I was standing he asked me what I was doing. Picking up one of the bullets that I had designed, I explained that I had just made a high speed long range bullet that could reach out to a thousand yards with killing force and leave no ballistics to be traced. With a blank look on his face, Tim simply said, "That is impossible". Pointing down range I handed Tim a pair of binoculars so he could watch as I fired. Sighting in my target I slowly pulled the trigger. There was a loud bang then I looked up at Tim's face, to see him standing there with his mouth opened in awe.

Looking at me Tim exclaimed "I can't believe that even made it that far and with that much accuracy, I saw half of the target explode when you hit it!"

Smiling back at him I said "It's all about how you make the product, and knowing how to use it."

Tim took one more look down range shaking his head, and remarked "Well it looks like you have it all down pat. Just remind me not to piss you off. From what I've seen, it doesn't look like I would even stand a chance in hell!"

Smiling at Tim I said "just don't get in the way of me and my target. I will take out anyone or anything that gets in my way so I can get my job done. We need to get back to the house so that we can get packed and ready to leave in the morning. We will be leaving about 4am so be ready or stay behind." Nodding in agreement Tim followed me back to the house. As we got to the house Sara informed us that lunch was ready and we needed to get washed up so we could eat.

After finishing lunch Tim and I went to get our things ready for the next day. As I packed, I could see the disappointment in Sara's eyes because I didn't have more time to spend with her and the kids. I too was feeling it, but I had to get my job taken care of. I was also feeling a lot of tension building up because as I worked to remove the price off our heads, I was building a reputation that was going to be hard to erase later down the road. I couldn't help but to wonder what would come of all this as time went on. I had to get my mind back to the task at hand. I didn't want to leave anything behind needed for the upcoming trip. After getting my clothes that I needed packed up, I grabbed my two special cases, taking them to my car first so I could pack them in the trunk. There was no way I was going to leave THEM behind. Going back in to get my rifle and clothes, I shouted at Tim to see if he was about done packing his stuff and loading it into the car, so we would be ready to go in the morning. Hollering back he responded that it would be just a couple of minutes and he would be out there, so I waited for Tim to get there with his stuff and get things arranged in the car. By the time I had all my stuff packed in, he was coming out the door with his bags. With that taken care of, I could now spend the rest of the afternoon with my wife and kids, before leaving for my job early in the morning.

It was about time for the kids to get home from school, and Sara was already in the kitchen starting dinner so we could eat a little early and get to bed. When the kids got home I made sure that they got all of their homework done before we went outside to play catch for a while, meanwhile dinner was being finished up. After playing outside for about an hour with the kids, Sara called out that dinner was ready, and for everyone to come in and get cleaned up. When I walked into the dining room I was surprised to only see three places set. Asking Sara what was up, she simply pointed towards the den where she had candles lit with dim lighting and only two plates set for me and her. Smiling I just nodded and headed that way. Sara went to the dining room said something to Tim, and then served them their plates. When I walked into the den I noticed that she had fixed up a very elegant dinner setting for me and her, along with music that was playing softly. She followed close behind me with our food, and sat it down on the table, then shut the door to the den so that there was no one there but us. We shared a very romantic dinner together, including some slow dancing, and just some good old quality time. We were really enjoying each other's company completely. After about two hours she gathered up our dishes and headed towards the kitchen, gathering the rest of the dishes along the way, and began cleaning up. She gave me a quick kiss, and then told me to tell the kids to get bathed and ready for bed. Winking at me she indicated that our romantic evening wasn't over yet, but we had to get the kids in bed first.

After we had got everything taken care of and the kids in bed, I noticed that she was acting a little different than usual. I asked her what was bothering her, and looking at me with sad eyes she said "I feel as if I am loosing you to this job. I know that I said before that I didn't mind if you took on this kind of job, but I am getting worried about you and the whole family. You are not the same person that used to be anymore. You seem to be changing into someone that has no feelings sometimes and doesn't care if you live or die as long as you get the job done. I know that you love me and the kids, but you have started to keep secrets, and that worries me too because I don't know how dangerous it is for me not to know. You are just not yourself anymore, every since you have been out there trying to get these contracts off of all of our heads. What if you manage to succeed and then someone else puts them back out there again? What are you going to do then?"

Not knowing exactly what to say, all I could tell her is that I would find a way to keep that from happening. Cuddling up close to her and wrapping my arms around her, her words continued running through my head. I could see her reasoning, but still there was no way that I could ever tell her everything without putting her and the kids in danger, or in a position that she wouldn't know how to handle. Damn this job! Why did I even get in to this? It was slowly destroying my whole life as I knew it, and replacing it with a new type of person that I never considered being. All I know now is that I have to get some sleep so that Tim and I could leave for our next job in the morning. Four o'clock would come early.

As the alarm went off the next morning at 3am, I reached over to turn it off, and Sara got up, put on her pretty satin robe that I loved to see her in, and went into the kitchen to start some coffee and breakfast for us, before we left to do our job one more time. Getting out of bed I went to take a quick shower before we ate, and I continued thinking about her question. As I stood in the shower lathering up, I realized that I couldn't tell her everything because I didn't know what 'everything' was, myself. Maybe I would know more if I manage to ever find that old witch that James had told me about, and had the opportunity to ask her these questions that were haunting me. After I had finished showering and drying off, I caught myself looking around at everything, wondering if I would ever see any of this again. Walking into the kitchen Sara was just finishing up breakfast and getting ready to serve it.

CHAPTER 4

After we finished eating Tim excused himself to check on a few last minute needs before the trip. Looking over at my beautiful wife, I told her that there was no way that I could really tell her everything because I didn't know all the answers yet myself, but as soon as I could, I would tell her.

She just nodded and replied "I understand" and smiled. Walking me out to the door she hugged me and I looked around at everything again one last time. Reaching the door I turned around, and looking into her eyes I could see all the love and concern she had, then I kissed her goodbye and told her everything would be alright, then headed to the car so that Tim and I could be on our way to Oklahoma.

As we got to the car, Tim looked over at me and asked "Do you want to drive first, or do you want me to take the wheel for a while?" I just waved him to the driver's side, and pointed down the road indicating for him to continue. I really didn't feel like driving right now. I had a lot on my mind and I needed to try and clear my head. After we had been on the road for about thirty minutes Tim asked me what I had on my mind because I wasn't acting normally. I replied to Tim "It's a lot of things. My family for one, and time away at work, and mostly not knowing exactly what I have gotten myself into, job included."

"Does any of it have to do with me being around?" Tim asked.

"No, it's nothing like that. It's kind of like some of the things that you have pointed out and asked me about. I don't know how to explain it, and it's starting to affect everything around me. The strange thing is that none of this ever happened until after my friend James died. I know of only one person that might be able to help me understand, but I have no idea how to get in touch with her. I have only met her once, but I didn't get a chance to ask any questions before she was gone." I said.

"Then why don't we go back to where you met her after we finish this job and maybe you can find her again so you can get the answers that you need?" Tim suggested.

"There are a few problems with that Tim. First I don't know her name or what she looks like. Secondly, she is everywhere and nowhere at all times. I have only heard her voice a few times. And third, from what I understand she died about a hundred years ago so I have to wait till she decides to contact me." I told him with a bewildered look on my face.

A strange look came over Tim's face as he asked "If she has been dead for over a hundred years, then how will you meet her or even communicate with her, and how is she going to get a hold of you?" Tim asked in a strange tone of voice.

Smiling at Tim I just said "James managed to get in touch with her but died before he could tell me how to get a hold of her myself. According to him, she is an old witch from the bayous of Louisiana. I'm not sure I believe in witches but it's the only thing that makes sense right now." I answered.

"You are freaking me out with this story. I am not sure whether or not to say if you are losing your mind or telling the truth, but I have seen a few strange things myself. I have some questions that I want answered too if you ever do get to talk to that witch again. Does what you keep in those two cases have anything to do with her or James?" Tim asked.

"No what I have in there came from a dream I had. I could have sworn that I was in space talking to aliens and they gave me the plans for them. At first I didn't think that it would work but then I went ahead and built them anyways, and found out that they worked better than I had ever expected. And before you ask, no there are not any written plans for them. I keep that all in my head so that no one else would be at risk for knowing what they are or what they can do." I informed him.

"That sounds great but what about you? Tim asked. If these weapons could cause the end of the world like you said, and the wrong person finds out, then everyone is at risk. Is that why you have been trying so hard to get the contracts removed ASAP?"

"No. These contracts were issued for a whole different reason, but it's just that I made the mistake of eliminating a bigger fish than I was led on to believe. Let's leave it at that for now." I said.

That's good, that's all I can take for now. How far should I drive before you take over?" Tim asked.

"We can switch when we reach Dallas, until then I am going to get some rest," Then I closed my eyes, and attempted to get some sleep for a while anyways.

Tim turned the radio on quietly and continued driving towards their destination. A few hours later, Tim woke me up as he pulled into a gas station, informing me that they were in Denton. "Good I said, let's get some coffee and something to eat after we fill up on gas, and then I'll take over from here."

"That sounds good to me. By the way, what were you dreaming about, do you remember? You were mumbling and twitching a lot, but I couldn't understand a word you were saying." Tim asked.

"No, I don't remember anything, but let's go eat, I'm hungry." I replied.

The gas station that we had pulled into had a small diner inside, so after we took turns relieving ourselves and washing up a little, we both sat down and looked at the menu, looking over what they had to offer. After choosing something that looked good, we ate, and then ordered coffee to go. It was time to get back on the road. As they settled in for the journey ahead, I advised Tim to get some rest, and that they would switch drivers again in Oklahoma City. Tim finished his coffee, then lowered his seat back, resting his head on the car door and closing his eyes, falling asleep shortly after.

As I continued down the road, my head was filled with hundreds of questions and scenarios of how this could end. Glancing into the rear view mirror, I saw that the Reaper was sitting in the back seat with us.

I spoke up saying "Hi James, glad you could join us." The Reaper nodded his head in response. "Hey by the way, before you disappear again, I need you to get in touch with that old witch for me. I really need to talk to her." I informed James. The Reaper nodded and faded away.

Tim sleepily lifted his head and opened his eyes, and asked me, "Who are you talking to?"

I turned my head slightly so I could look Tim in the eyes and replied, "You don't want to know, but it's a part of my curse." Tim nodded his acknowledgment, then laid his head back down and closed his eyes, drifting off back to sleep.

The next thing Tim knew, they were pulling into a truck stop in Oklahoma City. I got out of the car and began pumping gas, and Tim made his way inside to hunt for a bathroom. Afterwards, I pulled the car around, parking in front of the gas station, on the diner side, and then I went inside to relieve myself, and find Tim.

Together they headed back into the diner, grabbing a menu on the way to a table. They both ordered their meal, making small talk as they waited for the waitress to bring them their food. They ate quietly, and then paid for their meal, leaving a generous tip for the waitress, and headed back out to the car. It was Tim's turn to drive. I made sure to tell Tim to wake me up when they reached Broken Bow, Oklahoma, being as how I was familiar with the area, and knew where we were going. Tim agreed, and then before handing Tim the car keys, I walked over to the trunk and pulled out a folder containing information about their upcoming mark, Johnny Mancini. I browsed through the files making sure that I committed to memory the details I needed to know to hunt down our mark and complete the job. If all went well, we would be able to do the job, and be on our way back home by tonight. When I got finished scanning over the files, I laid the folder in the back seat, and then closed my eyes so I could get a little more rest before the fun began.

As Tim reached the city limits of Broken Bow Oklahoma, he woke me up from my sleep, and then he searched for a place to get gas. After finding a place, he turned the keys back over to me, so I could take over from there. I groggily opened my eyes and got out, making my way inside to pay for the gas, and get some coffee. As I returned with two coffees in hand, I told Tim to take the time to go over the files as well, so he would be completely familiarized with the case and what had to be done.

They spent half the day searching the local area that Johnny is known to hang out at, and finally caught a glimpse of him leaving a nearby restaurant. He appeared to be in a hurry, while talking on his cell phone. Johnny jumped into his car and sped away at a rapid speed.

Tim looked over at me, and said "Damn, we just missed him."

"Not yet," I replied, and then pulled out at a safe distance to follow their target. After pursuing the other car for around 15 minutes, I spoke up saying, "It looks like he is leaving town, things couldn't get better." They continued following for about another 10 miles outside of town, then slowed down as they watched their target pull into what appeared to be an abandoned farmhouse. The place was a mess, and had obviously been unused for several years. Nearly every window had been broken, and the grass was waist high, leaving a cold abandoned feeling in its wake.

Both Tim and I looked at each other, both wondering the same question. What was Johnny doing here? I continued driving a short way, pausing on the other side a small hill, and then putting the car in park, they both stepped out, stretching their legs, and observing the entire area. They needed to make sure that this would be as good as any place to do what they had come to do. First making sure that they were alone, and would remain that way, I walked around to the trunk of the car, and grabbed my rifle and special bullets. Then they both slipped through the fence surrounding the property, which was no hard feat, as the fence was falling apart anyways, and then crouched down in the tall grass, sneaking their way to the crest of the hill, so they could scout the area, and keep eyes on their target as I got everything set up. It took me all of 5 minutes to get everything ready, then I handed Tim the binoculars, and told him to locate our target, and keep his eyes on him. After a few minutes went by, Tim asked me, "What are we waiting for, isn't this the perfect chance to get it done?"

I looked up at Tim with a wary look on my face, and said, "He is up to something, probably here to meet someone, so I want to wait and see who he is meeting, and why out here in the middle of nowhere."

They didn't have to wait long for an answer, after about 15 minutes, a white Ford Crown Victoria pulled into the unkempt driveway, and parked behind Johnny's car. A tall, dark well built man with balding hair stepped out of the car, and made his way toward Johnny. Taking the binoculars from Tim, I zoomed in on my target and the new arrival. After a minute or two, a smile crept over my face, and Tim asked, "What are you smiling about?"

I handed the binoculars back to Tim, nodding my head in their direction. "I'm glad we waited," I told him. "Not only is our target here, but that is Cisco Vargas that just pulled up, from the old gang. He is one of the targets I have been looking for."

It appeared like the two of them were arguing about something; their loud voices could be heard faintly over the meadow, just not quite loud enough to catch what they were saying. "We may only have enough time to get one of them, and right now Johnny is at the top of that list." Tim said. "Not necessarily," I responded.

"That is at least 3000 yards away, with two targets there is simply no way," Tim said. As they continued to argue, I continued watching through the scope of my rifle. Then Cisco got in Johnny's face yelling about something, and poking him in the chest, using his finger. I fired, striking Johnny in the back of the head, and taking out both targets at the same time. At a closer look, the bullet had entered the back of Johnny's skull, exiting his left nostril, and striking Cisco in the center of his heart. Looking out across the field where the pair had fallen, I started to smile as an ice cold wind blew across my back. Then, there was the Reaper himself collecting the souls of the two dead men and giving me a thumb up. I was a little envious that Tim was unable to see what I was seeing or what was happening, or feel the cold chill of death itself as I could. Looking through his binoculars, with an expression of awe on his face, Tim said excitedly, "I have never seen a shot so amazing! I would have never thought it possible to make that shot so accurate at such a distance!"

I looked up and smiled. "I told you that the rounds I made are very special, and you will never find these for sale anywhere." With that said, I got up and picked up my rifle and equipment and then headed back towards the car. This job was done, and it was time to start on the next job that Rudy would have in store for us.

On the way back to the car I heard a shrill crackling voice of an old woman saying, "soon our time will come and all will be explained." Then as the voice faded away in the breeze I could hear her laughing in an eerie tone. Taking a quick look around I only saw Tim walking towards the car. Nodding to myself, I knew that it was the old witch talking, and I welcomed her voice, and waited for that time to come.

CHAPTER 5

Walking down the hill was a lot easier than it was to go up, and it did give a great view of the road so we could see if anyone was coming from any direction. Once I reached the car, I gave one last look around before putting my equipment away, thinking about how grateful I was that this was a dead area, with little to no traffic. As we were leaving, I listened in as Tim was on his cell phone talking with Rudy, explaining the details of how their last job just went down. I was particularly amused when I heard Tim bragging about the expertise of the shot, and the radical distance, and extreme luck of hitting both targets with one shot. Then after a short pause, Tim went on to explain who the second target was, and why he was taken out as well. He then went on to ask if there was any tasks pending right away, or whether or not they could just go on home from there. He waited briefly for a response, and then hung up the phone.

Looking over at me, Tim informed me that Rudy had directed us to just hang around somewhere close by while he checked to make sure that there was nothing else for us to do in this area. I agreed, but mentioned that they ought to find a hotel outside of the county line just in case, so he began to drive in the direction of Choctaw County, pulling up in Hugo, at a cheap motel. Tim headed into the office to get a room for the night, thinking to himself that tomorrow would tell if they were going home, or on to another job somewhere else. After settling into the room I turned on the television so I could hear if there was any news about our recent job. The six o'clock news mentioned nothing of interest to either one of them. Oh well, it was still early and they were both hungry by now anyways. There had to be a restaurant or café somewhere close by.

As Tim and I entered the office at the motel to get directions on somewhere to get a good meal, we noticed the desk clerk intently listening to a police scanner. Looking up as we entered, the desk clerk started walking up to the counter shaking his head from side to side chuckling. Reaching the counter he remarked, "Those idiots in that other county done went and lost track of another cop and they are trying to find him."

I grinned and replied, "Must happen a lot around here if it doesn't alarm you that much," as Tim just stood by and listened.

"Oh only about once a month, and now, what can I do for you?" the desk clerk asked.

"My friend and I are not from this area and were wondering where we might be able to find us a good meal" I said. After getting some advice and directions, Tim and I took off walking towards the café that the clerk had recommended. There was no use driving since it was only a few blocks away, and we both could use the exercise, being as how we had been spending far too much time sitting in the car lately.

As we made our way toward the café, Tim spoke up saying, "Can you believe that a cop is missing and nobody seems worried about it? This must be a real backwards place."

"Yeah it is, but there are worse things than that. You should have been around when I was training with James. You wouldn't have believed half of the drama that was constantly going on back then," I responded.

"You should tell me about it sometime, maybe I could understand a little more about what's going on inside that head of yours." Tim said.

"Like I said, you would have had to have been there. I'm not even too sure myself." And then just as they turned the corner to the café, I stopped talking immediately, standing very still and staring straight ahead with my mouth slightly ajar. Tim turned and looked in the same direction that I was staring, but all that he could see was a vacant street, with a sign marking the café that they were supposed to be heading towards. What I was seeing was James the Reaper, my old friend. He was standing beside the old witch, the one that I had been searching for, still looking to find the answers that I needed to understand what was going on in my own head. After a few moments, I quickened my pace, almost to a run, trying to get to them before they disappeared again. But as I got nearer, the two of them just got further and further away and then simply disappeared yet again. But I did hear the old witch, very loud and clear in her crackly voice saying, "Be patient, it's still not time for you to have the answers you are seeking just yet, but they will come sooner than you think." Then she started laughing again as her voice faded.

Coming to a dead stop, I looked over at Tim, because he had grabbed a hold of my arm, and was shaking it, trying to get my attention, while he himself was panting, also out of breath, and asking, "What the hell is going on, are you losing it, or is there something going on that I should be worried about?"

"No, I'm good, lets just get to the café and get us some food, I am about to starve." I told Tim.

"You could have fooled me, you sped right past the place over a block ago. You didn't even slow down, you just went right on by it, like it wasn't even there. Let's turn back around and head back, and no more of this weird stuff, okay?" Tim asked in a concerned tone of voice. Nodding in agreement, we turned around, and I told Tim that I could use a drink. Once inside, they ordered their meal, and I sat there thinking intensely, as Tim kept a close eye on me, wondering what was really going on inside my head. The meal went by with an eerie silence between us both, and after finishing our meal, we started our walk back to the motel. Neither of us dared to say a word, so we both just walked back slowly and silently, both of us seemingly deep in thought. Once in our room, I went over and sat down on my bed, thinking and trying to make sense of the earlier incident. After about twenty minutes Tim finally spoke up, asking about what it was that I had seen.

"Paul, tell me the truth; do I need to call Rudy, and tell him that you need some time off, or are you going to be okay? I really need to know that you are going to be ok, and that these occurrences aren't going to affect our business. The last thing either one of us needs is to be locked up in some jail cell, or psychiatric hospital out here in some backwoods town, with no way to get help or get home." Tim asked concerned.

"For one thing, I would not be in a jail cell or psychiatric hospital anywhere," I informed him. "Now as far as anything else going on, it's my own private business, and no, it will not affect anything that I have to get done. So to answer your question, no you don't have to call anyone. If you don't feel comfortable being out here with me, then hand me over a final pass and I will continue on alone. The jobs I am getting through Rudy are helping me find the people that I am looking for, in order to remove these contracts off of Sara and the kids' heads. But as far as the pay, I don't really need the money. Sara and I were left a substantial amount from an unidentified source. And before you ask, the amount is not up for discussion."

"Well from what I've seen so far, I would say it was quite a lot," Tim smirked as he displayed a devilish grin. "But I would still like to know what you are going through as my brother in law, not as an evaluator, or boss, or whatever you want to call it. I still have my sister and niece and nephew to worry about also. You are carrying a lot of secrets with you and I would like to know that none of them is going to affect their well being. Sara has even commented to me, that she is afraid that you might be having some kind of a breakdown or mental overload." Tim said.

"Well, I will admit that since James's death, things have been a bit crazy for me. I myself am not sure exactly what is going on, but I do know that I am not losing my mind in any way, fashion, or form. I do have to figure out what all this means before it gets out of control and it becomes too late to do anything about, and I'm working on that now. Don't think I'm crazy, but I will tell you one thing. As you know, it was fabled that James rode with the Reaper. Now he IS the Reaper, and he rides with me. That explains some of the unexplainable faces you've seen while you've been riding with me." I informed him.

Turning a ghostly pale color, Tim asked me in a nervous whisper, "Are you telling me that death is riding around with us?"

"Yes, that's exactly what I'm saying, and I alone am the only one that knows about his presence here with us. That's all you need to know for now, so let's get some rest, we have a long day ahead of us tomorrow." Due to the day's events, I had a rough night though, tossing and turning, unable to get much rest. Tim didn't rest any better than I did, his mind kept replaying what I had told him about the Reaper, and his presence among us. After what seemed like an eternity, Tim finally fell asleep, only to be woken up early that morning by me, informing him that it was time to pack up and go, effective immediately. And to be quick about it.

As Tim sluggishly got to his feet, he asked what was going on. "They found the bodies, and a detective from Dallas is heading our way. And I know exactly who it is." I informed him worriedly.

While getting dressed, Tim asked me, "Well, who is it, and how would you know him?" The morning news did confirm that a detective from Dallas was headed our way, to help out with the Mancini case.

"One of the last tasks that I did for James was to mail a file to a detective Brown in Dallas, and I think that same detective is the one headed this way. According to James, this detective was like a bloodhound after his butt for five years, up until he died. And if it IS detective Brown that's headed our way like I think it is, then we don't need to be anywhere around here when he arrives."

"So now where are we going from here?" Tim asked on the way out to the car.

Placing the key in the ignition I just sat there for a few moments and then I replied, "To Dallas. I have a place there where we can wait this out a bit, and not draw any attention to Sara and the kids. While we are there we can also go and see Raul, and maybe spend some time fishing. Or whatever, we'll figure it out when we get there, unless of course you have something better in mind for us to do, because right now, until I know more, we don't need to go home."

"That sounds good to me, but I would like to know why we are running and hiding just because a detective from Dallas is heading this way, and you're not even sure if it's him yet." Tim spoke up.

Firing up the Charger, I started thinking about how to explain to Tim just how serious this situation could be. After about thirty miles out of town, I started to tell Tim what I did know about what was going on. "I will answer your question from earlier. You said you wanted to know more about what is going on, and what I'm aware of at this time, but this info goes no farther than this car. Understood?" Tim nodded his agreement. "First off, Detective Brown is more than just a police detective. He is also a high ranking military official. I know this, because when Sara was working for the DOD lab, he was always there, and held a level seven security clearance. You might not think that's important, but even the president only holds a level six clearance. There are some things that even the president is not allowed to have knowledge of, or access to. It makes it easier for political deniability. I am not sure what kind of relation he and James had, or didn't have, nor do I know what was in the files that he had me send off contained, but Brown is also the one that handed Sara the list of who was involved in our house bombing, and the hit list. That's how I know who I am looking for. While I was making what I have in my cases, he almost got a hold of my research and test data on one occasion that I was using in the manufacturing. He is a lot smarter then he lets on, and I don't need him snapping at my heels, or getting involved in any way. And before you ask, YES, he has access to data and weapons that even the president doesn't even know exists. That's one of the things that makes him so dangerous." I informed Tim.

"Who is this DOD that you are talking about? All I know is that Sara was working for a medical science lab there in Dallas?" Tim inquired.

Giving a sigh, I began to explain what I could. "Well she did work for a medical science lab, but it was the Department of Defense bio chemical warfare division. Your sister was making viruses and chemicals to use during war, to take out the enemy on a large scale basis. I do know that one of the things that she made took out a whole town in a matter of hours." Glancing over at Tim, I noticed that his face had turned ghost white, with a blank expression.

Tim sat there speechless for about ten miles, and then looked over at me and in a trembling voice remarked, "Those are the people that are even worse than us; they can make anyone that they choose to disappear from ever even existing. Like, I mean no birth records, no school records or any other trace that would prove that that person ever existed, including friends and family. I had no ideal that you and my sister were involved with people of such power. Are you sure that James wasn't a part of them too?" Tim inquired.

Shrugging my shoulders I simply responded, "I didn't get to stay with him long enough to find out for sure. All I know is that James always had some very high up targets, which no regular hit man would ever even attempt to take on. I do know that he was involved in some other stuff that bears no explanation as well, and there is no way to logically explain what was going on. As far as I can see it right now, we are on this merry go round for the entire ride and it is not stopping until the bell tolls for us both, or the rides is over. Like it or not, you are now on this ride with us too, but at least you have the choice to get off at any time you wish, for now. Sara still has that option as well, and I won't let it get to the point where that option changes at all, at anytime, for any reason. But as for me, the ride has already started, and there is no escape or getting off at this point in the game, my fate is already sealed." I said.

"What are you talking about Paul?" Tim asked. "You have done an amazing job at concealing and covering up our identities, and getting us out of the situations we have been in with no problems. You still have a chance to get out without a trace leading back to you or Sara." Tim commented.

"I wish. What about Dallas where I took out Downhill? There was no way that anyone except a real pro that could have done that. And then there was that witness that saw my car even though he couldn't see inside the car through the tinted windows, so I know there is still a report somewhere. Then we have Detective Brown who gave the list of names to Sara and now those people are coming up dead too. As far as the report goes, there was only one figure seen in the car. Sara was not in town, and you were with Raul, so that clears the both of you completely. And to make things even more complicated, now they have the evidence of my advanced weapon that was used on the job, and had yet to been seen before by anyone else. Also if Brown is the blood hound that I think he is there is no way he is just going to sweep all this under the carpet and forget about it." I told him.

"When you put it that way, I suppose you are stuck on this ride now. What would you do if worse case scenario Sara becomes inevitably involved?" Tim asked.

"Like I said, I will not allow that to happen, no matter what I have to do to make sure it stays that way." I responded in an aggravated tone. "Also, you need to call Rudy and let him know that we are changing our location and heading back to Dallas."

"By the way, how many more people do you have run through before you can get the contracts off Sara and the kids now? And are we going to that lavish condo you own in Dallas to stay? You do know that one day you are going to have to tell me how you managed to afford such a place out in west Texas, along with a condo too in Dallas, when you and Sara were struggling to make it not that long ago. If we ARE going back to that same condo we must go back to that little café we went to the last we were there. That waitress there looked awfully nice, and the food was also great, but I can't remember her name," Tim rambled on. I could tell he was nervous because he couldn't shut up, just one of his little quirks he had that I had learned to put up with.

As soon as Tim shut up long enough for me to answer his questions, I began to give him the answers as best as I could. "I still have three more to go, and they will be the most difficult to get rid of. And yes, we are going back to that condo to stay a while until it is safe, or we get another job to do. As far as to how I got the condo, it was part of the big windfall that I got along with the place in west Texas. That's all I will say about that and yes we will go back to the café where Alice works. You might want to be careful about whom you are trying to seduce though; they might not share the same view as to our chosen profession as we do. That could be dangerous to you in a number of ways, not to mention all the days and nights you won't be home with her. Just ask your sister about all the nights alone she has had to put up with since I got into this business. I am the best because I was trained by the best but I got something that I didn't bargain for, not even in my wildest dreams. And even now sometimes I wonder if what I have to deal with is worth it or not. I do have this odd feeling that when I do finally find out what is going on, it's not going to be good at all for anyone involved."

"Sounds like good advice, but that doesn't mean that I can't do a little fishing on the side, it might be worth it. But since we are close by the Oklahoma border, I think I should call Rudy and get him caught up on everything that's going on." Tim responded. With that, Tim called Rudy's cell phone number, and after Rudy answered the phone, Tim began to catch Rudy up on everything he needed to know. After finishing his call with Rudy, Tim said "I've got good news; Chris Gynas was seen near Kill Devil Hills, yesterday evening."

"Oh really, where exactly did they say they spotted him?" I asked.

"On the beach over at Middletown Lake Landing. Maybe we should go see the beach ourselves over that way sometime soon," Tim responded.

"You're right, maybe we should. I'm even tempted to go check it out now! But by the time we get there, he'll probably be gone, so it would most likely be a waste of time and effort to try and catch up with him at this moment. But don't worry, we will catch him, make no mistake about that. And I guarantee he will wish he had never taken on the contract to try and take out my family. I have special plans for him when we meet." I told Tim. With that said Tim seemed to settle down and start to enjoy the rest of the trip back to Dallas.

Once we reached the condo Tim was anxious to get up to it. I couldn't help but chuckle when I heard Tim as he walked over to the sixty inch flat screen telling it how much he had missed it as he turned it on. Now all we had to do was wait and see how things went so that I could plan out our next move. Taking out my phone I called Sara to inform her of what was going on and tell her that we were good for now and that there was no need to worry. After getting the news from home on how she and the kids were doing I went in the kitchen to see what we had there to snack on. Making myself a sandwich I asked Tim if he would like one also, to hold him over till we went to get dinner later and he could see Alice again. Tim answered back yes with a grin on his face at the thought of being able to have another shot at trying to get her to go out with him. Although in my head I didn't see it happening, but it was fun to watch and listen. Sitting in front of the television we watched the noon day news to see if there was any news about the Oklahoma job, especially any news of Detective Brown. The only thing mentioned was that there was a cop shot and killed and that an out of state detective was brought in to help out with the case.

The afternoon passed by quickly I noticed Tim hurrying to get cleaned up and make himself presentable before we went to the diner. When Tim had finally got ready we headed out to the car, and Tim looked over at me and asked "Why are you taking your two cases with us to dinner? Is what's in them so important that they can't be left alone locked up?"

"Yes they are that important and I don't want to be caught without them should the need arise that I actually did need them. What you don't understand is that what's in these cases could change the world as you know it overnight. It would be worse to be caught without them then it will be to get caught with them. That's also why I have retinal scan locks on the cases so that they will only unlock for me." I told Tim in a serious tone.

"Damn, if they are that good then you could go public and make a fortune selling them in mass production." Tim commented.

"Yeah, and end the world in the same step. What I have will never be allowed to be sold to the general public because the government won't allow it to happen, then me and everyone that has any knowledge of them will vanish off the face of the earth. There are times that I wish that I had failed in my quest to make them but, that's too late now. Just like with Pandora, the box is open now and there is no way to put it all back in once it's out. Besides if at any time you don't feel comfortable with me then you know what to do." I remarked.

"Well Rudy said that we are still stuck together for at least another couple of jobs before he will consider putting you up as a self employed independent contractor through the team. Besides I thought we were going to dinner not a debate, but as far as I'm concerned you are ready to go now. You haven't needed any help from me or anyone else since you started. Now let's go eat." Tim said laughingly.

Nodding my head in agreement I pointed towards the door. It was comical watching Tim practice his lines as we were heading to the café. As I watched him I kept replaying how I met Sara and then I remembered that I broke one of her main rules that she sat for me to follow when I first started this business. Now I am wondering what kind of consequence I was going to have to pay later on. She had set two rules for me when I started and that was never get caught alive and don't bring the job home. Well the job hit home, and now I had to do my best to get it away from home. The sad thing is that when I get it all cleared up will trouble stay away or, will there be a whole new set of crap show up? That had to be determined later, we were already at the café and it was time for my amusement. Alice noticed us pulling in and was waiting for us when we entered the door with two iced teas and two coffees, asking us if we needed the back seats or not. Shaking my head no she sat us near the middle of the room.

"Little late in the evening for you two isn't it?" Alice asked as she sat out the menus. "I'll be back shortly to take your order." she said as she turned around and left to attend to some other customers.

Looking over at Tim I commented grinning, "Looks like you are going to have a hard time since it looks like Alice is the only waitress tonight."

Scuffing at my comment Tim just continued to look over the menu. When Alice returned, I placed my order and then Tim placed his order saying, "Along with your phone number so that maybe we could go and get a drink sometime."

Alice took our order and without a hitch told Tim, "I don't date a man that travels for a living and most importantly I don't think my husband and three kids will approve of it, but you are more than welcome to ask him if you'd like," With that she went to turn our orders in and I smirked at the look on Tim's face as she walked away. It was all I could do to not burst out laughing as Tim sat there with his mouth hanging open.

After dinner was done Tim and I went back to my place so we could settle down for the night. While Tim went to his room to lick his wounds from the earlier rejection I decided that I would watch a little TV and maybe catch some of the news. Just as the news was coming on I heard Tim's phone ring, and I tried to listen in but the voice was too muffled to hear what Tim was saying. I didn't have long to wait though, because Tim appeared in the doorway announcing that Rudy had called and that we had another job to do. The good thing is that we had a month to do it, but the bad thing is that it was in Billings Montana. Rudy would call tomorrow with more information on the person we would be after and anything else he had on this person.

CHAPTER 6

Looking over at Tim, I just told him that we would worry about that tomorrow, and that we needed to get all the rest that we could tonight because we might be leaving tomorrow sometime.

When morning came around Tim and I sat at the table eating the breakfast that I had cooked for us, and drinking coffee when his phone went off. After sliding him a notebook and pen, he began writing down the information that was being given to him by Rudy. When he finished writing he got up from the table and walked to the other side of the room so that I couldn't hear what was being said and continued his conversation with Rudy.

Coming back to the table Tim said, "Damn you must have made a good impression on Rudy because this time we have a high profile official to deal with. I was asking him if he really wanted us to do this job and he said that he feels like you are the only one that can get it done without being caught. The person we are going after is Matt Hemsley. He is a United States governor that is in the running for U.S. senator. Looks like you finally got your status for the higher profile targets a little sooner than we both expected. He didn't have a whole lot on him at this time so we will have to go and do our own research and determine the best way to handle this." Tim announced.

Looking up at Tim from my plate I simply told him, "Don't be so worried, I will handle this job just as well as I have handled the others before it. There won't be any mistakes or slip ups and in the end Mr.

Hemsley will be just as dead as the rest. Oh, and enjoy the rest of the day because we will be leaving for Billings in the morning." I smiled at him and then returned to my breakfast.

It was sad but, the only thing I could think of at that time was how proud James would have been to know that I had climbed the ladder so fast because of his training. Feeling a cold chill I looked up and there he was just standing there, as he noticed I saw him he just nodded his head as if to say good job I knew you could do it and vanished.

The rest of the day went by pretty uneventful except for packing for the trip, and making reservations so we would have a place to stay at. Checking over my weapons, I made sure that they were in good working order. My power cells that powered my guns were still at full charge so there was no need to worry there. As I got everything ready to go I sat it by the door so that I could take it down and get it situated in the car before morning except for my guns, they stayed with me until we were leaving. Tim, noticing what I was doing began to do the same so that there would be no delay in leaving when morning came around. Pulling out a map I began to plan out our route that we were going to take, and then I showed Tim since he would be helping in the driving. With that done it was getting late, so I told Tim that we were going somewhere that we could get us a good steak dinner and no "Alice" wasn't part of it.

Finding a good steak house we went inside grabbed a menu and sat down. When the waitress came over I told Tim that he could order anything that he wanted in celebration of the promotion that we just got. I ordered myself a 16oz. ribeye steak with a baked potato and fried pickles, while Tim ordered himself a top sirloin with fries and we both had iced tea to drink. As the waitress walked away, I looked over at Tim and asked him, "Why don't you try to get her phone number?"

"Hell no! She's old enough to be my mama, and by the looks of it, she has to weigh at least 300Lbs or more." Tim answered with a disgusted look on his face.

Laughing out loud I responded with, "That probably means she is single and available."

After that remark Tim had a disgusted look on his face until dinner was finally brought to us. After enjoying our celebration dinner we went back to the condo for a good rest before heading out to Billings in the morning. Setting my alarm for five am, we took turns at showering and getting ready for tomorrow, it would be our last chance to complete our hygiene for about two days. But for now we were going to take advantage of the amenities that we had. A nice, hot shower, a full belly and a comfortable bed; what else could anyone need.

As the alarm went off I got up and started the coffee, then knocked on Tim's door to wake him up and inform him that it was time to get dressed and leave, then I went back to my room to get dressed. We both came out about the same time and went towards the coffee pot to get some. I poured two cups and took mine to the table while Tim grabbed his cup.

Sitting down Tim asked, "No breakfast today?"

Shaking my head from side to side I just said "No, we will get something later on, when we stop for gas."

Taking a sip from his cup Tim replied, "Good because I am not hungry this early in the morning anyway. Besides we don't need the dirty dishes we would have to wash to slow us down.

As we drank our coffee, Tim could see that I had something on my mind from the far away look in my eyes. Looking straight at me Tim asked, "What's wrong, are you having second thoughts about this job? If you don't feel comfortable with this job I can call Rudy back and tell him that you would rather not take this job.

"It's not that; I was just thinking about the last time that I was in Billings I got a call from James informing me that he had sent me the wrong way on purpose and to say good bye. That's when I was told to open the letter that he had given me to hold on to for him, and also had to deliver the letter he had given me, to deliver to his ex-wife. I did my best but when I tried to deliver it, she would not have anything to do with it; she wouldn't even open it just told me that whatever was in it now belonged to me. Also, that I should consider my obligation to bring it filled because I did my part and it has been refused, and since I couldn't return it to sender, to enjoy whatever was inside as she closed the door. Now before you ask, no, it is not going to affect the job in any way, it's just the last memory I have of James." I said distantly.

"Sorry I had no idea, but like you said it's just a memory and as long as it does not have any affect on the job we are good." Tim said as he was washing out the coffee pot and our cups.

Grabbing my two cases from my bedroom I told Tim that we needed to get on the road, so that we could get this done. Looking back at me Tim stated that one of these days I was going to have to show him what is so secretive about the cases that I always carry around. Shaking my head I informed Tim again that if he was to ever find out what I had here that he would become a permanent target to the feds as well as other members of this organization. It was best if he never knows what I am carrying around because it is my cross to bear and I don't want to put it on anyone else's back. With that we both walked out, and I made a last look around before shutting the door. We had packed everything that we would need in the car the day before, except the cases that I had to put in, so it was pretty simple to get going from this point.

Leaving out, I took first drive while Tim got a little more sleep. We would change drivers and get some breakfast up around Lubbock.

Turning on the radio I put on some music to drive by while Tim examined the inside of his eyelids. After a few hours I noticed we were approaching Lubbock and was in need of gas, so I reached over and nudged Tim awake, and informed him to wake up, we were going to be stopping soon to get gas, food and switch drivers, so he needed to wake up now. Yawning and stretching Tim slowly started to wake up telling me that it was about time, because he was now hungry. Finding a truck stop on the outside of town, I pulled in and started to fill up as Tim made his way to the restaurant, where I would meet up with him after I finished filling up the gas.

When I walked into the restaurant Tim was already sitting at a table and had coffee and tea waiting along with a menu to look at. Looking over the menu we made our choice then motioned for the waitress to come take our order. While we were waiting for our food, Tim inquired as to where we were at so that he would know which way he needed to go after we got back out on the road. I told him we had just gone through Lubbock and that he needed to head on to New Mexico and up to Colorado and we would change drivers again there. Nodding in agreement, Tim said that he would have no problem with that.

Leaving out of the truck stop, I settled in for a nice relaxing ride for the next couple of hours. Its not often I get to just sit back and look at the beauty of nature and the farm animals with nothing on my mind, or anything to do as I went by them. So for the next few hours I just sat back and watched. As time flew by, I started to doze off, and by the time I woke up, we were already in Trinidad Colorado.

Tim was pulling into a truck stop just outside of town, so we could fill the car up again, and relieve ourselves. After that we checked out the café there for lunch. We sat down and ate a brief lunch, then ordered a couple of drinks to go, and we decided to switch drivers while we were stopped, so that Tim could get some rest now.

I got behind the wheel, and got back on the freeway, and I let Tim know that our next stop wouldn't be until we got to Montana. So if he wanted to get some shut eye, now would be a good time to catch a few hours rest. Tim nodded his head in agreement, and adjusted his seat so he could lean back, and moved around a bit until he found a comfortable position, then started snoring shortly after.

The drive for the most part was uneventful, until we reached Steamboat Springs, Colorado. Pulling off the exit, and stopping at a red light, I noticed a car that pulled up beside me. Looking over, I noticed that Chris Gynas was driving the car beside me. What was he doing around here, I wondered to myself? I was grateful that the windows of the car were tinted extremely dark, so that no one could look in from outside, which gave me the advantage, at least for the moment.

Since we were a little ahead of schedule and not in any rush, I decided to follow him around a bit, to see what I could find out about what he was doing here. As I was tailing him around town, Tim woke up, and asked if we had already made it to Montana yet. Without looking away from the car I was tailing, I told him no, not yet, but since we were making such good time, I decided to take a small detour for a few days. But I told him that we would get there on time, not to get worried about it. Tim asked "What do you mean, a small detour?"

"The car in front of us is Chris Gynas, and I want to find out what he is doing here, and where he is going." I told Tim. "I'm not sure if I can do anything about him right now, but I want to check it out and see if I can." Coming to a railroad crossing, the warning flashers for the train started blinking, indicating that a train was coming, and the gate came down as well. I noticed the train was moving at a high speed as it passed in front of me. Once it had passed through and the track cleared again, Chris continued on for about another mile or so, and then turned into a drive way off the main road we were on. Memorizing the address, I kept on driving so as not to draw attention, then backtracked to the town courthouse to look up some records.

Looking up the address at the court house, I discovered that the house there belonged to his mother. Perfect, I thought to myself, he is going to be here for a while anyways. Now I needed to get information on the local train schedules, while I was here. I discovered that the train we had to wait on just a little while ago, passed the same way everyday, at the same time. Thinking to myself, I figured if he passed the same way everyday and time as well, I might be able to come up with a plan.

I left the court house and walked back to the car where Tim was waiting, and I informed him that due to the new circumstances, I was going to arrange for us to stay in town here for a few days. I told him that we were not avoiding or changing the plans we already had, just moving them back a little so I could kill two birds with one stone so to speak. I was going to have to look for Chris anyways, he just happened to fall into my lap, so I wasn't going to complain. I would much rather take advantage of my luck, and use it wisely.

Nodding his agreement, Tim responded that it was no big deal. They still had a month to do what they had come this way to do, so it wasn't going to be a problem if we took care of other business on the way there. With that agreed upon, we both were hungry, so we started looking around to see what our options were going to be for dinner.

We found a small restaurant that sounded good, so we got some dinner, and while we were waiting on our food to be brought out, Tim was asking the waitress if she knew any local decent hotels or inns close by that she would recommend. She gave them a couple local names, and general locations, and she also gave her number to Tim. Who accepted it with a giant grin on his face. Looking across the table at me, Tim said, "At least I'll be able to look her up if we ever pass through here again. But if we do, you're on your own next trip."

Looking back at him I told him, "I totally agree because I already have what I want and I am not looking to mess things up. Now back to finding us a place to stay while we are here. This place here looks like a good spot. It's right here on the same route to Chris's moms' house. Depending on what room we get I might be able to keep tabs on his comings and goings from right here without him even noticing." Calling up the motel, I inquired if they had any rooms available with a view of the road. Surprisingly, he told me that he had three rooms like that, and that I could have my pick of them when I got there to check in.

When we got through eating, we decided to find some where to put gas in the car again, just to be on the safe side since we were not familiar with this area. Once we located the hotel, we pulled in, and asked for the manager that I had spoken to a short while ago. He appeared a few minutes later, and offered for us to follow him so he could show us the rooms. Picking the one with the best view of the direction I was most interested in, I accompanied the manager back to the front to pay the tab for a few days. The manager offered me a discount if I paid a few days up front, because these rooms were not very often occupied as it was. With that taken care of, Tim and I grabbed whatever essentials we would need for the night and went inside our room.

Once inside, we picked our beds, and then put what few things we brought inside away, getting settled in. After I made sure my two special cases were stowed away, I claimed first shower, and picked out a change of clothes, while Tim was flipping through the channels on the TV looking for something interesting to watch.

I took my time in the shower, allowing the hot water to run over my body. It helped my muscles relax somewhat after sitting on my butt for the last several hours. After I was finished, I got out and went to the bedroom to change, allowing Tim to go ahead and get his shower as well, before it got too late. Then as I was towel drying my hair, I flipped on the local news, trying to get a feel for the town, and the overall mood of the area. I waited for Tim to finish up in the shower, before turning down the lights, and settling down for bed. We were both exhausted and it didn't take long before we were both out of it, competing to see who could snore the loudest.

I woke up early the next morning just as the sun was rising, and stepping out side the door, I got a glimpse of Chris heading down the highway. I casually walked over to the hotel office, and inquired about their knowledge if any, of the Gynas family that supposedly lived here in this area. The guy on duty at the front desk replied that he was familiar with the name. He said they even owned a hardware store not too far from there. He also said that he wasn't fond of the place really, but now that the owners son had returned, he avoids the place altogether because the guy was a rude asshole when he was in charge. I thanked him for sharing with me what little he knew, and then I asked him where it was, so I could avoid it. After getting the information I asked for, I returned to my room and decided it was a good time to wake Tim up.

After I got Tim to wake up, I told him to go ahead and get dressed. I suggested that we head into town for some breakfast and to do some investigating here and there. There were a couple of places on my mind I wanted to check out.

Tim nodded his approval, and then inquired as to whether or not he should bring anything specific for this trip. "No," I responded. "Not for this trip. We are doing more reconnaissance than anything else for right now. I just want to get a sense of the area, and where certain places are located so that I'm not running around blind here. Especially if the need to run or hide became necessary," I informed him. "I like to know what my options are before I need them, rather than last minute. That is the biggest mistake you can make in this line of work."

We got into the car and headed towards town. We stopped at one of the local café's closer to us, and ordered breakfast. When the waitress came back with our food, I decided to ask if she knew how to get to the address that I showed her on a piece of paper. Looking at the address she nodded and began telling me how to get there. I thanked her for the information and we finished off breakfast while leaving her a generous tip for her help when we left.

Getting in the car I began telling Tim "what I need you to do is to go into this hardware store and look for this guy here in this picture I have on my phone. Don't try to do anything just see if he is there and ask one of the employees there if they know what time he leaves. Then come back out to me and I will formulate a plan of action on that information.

Please don't be a dumb ass this is not the time or place to start anything at all. I can't go in there because he knows me and he might recognize me, and I don't want to cause any panic in him right now."

Tim nodded in agreement and we started off for Gynas hardware store in downtown. Once we got there I parked about a block away and Tim got out and walked on up to the place. Once inside Tim called me on video chat and placed it in his shirt pocket so that I could see what was going on. I muted my phone so that there would be no accidental noise to give anything away and just watched and listened. As Tim walked through the aisles I caught a glimpse of Chris at the register arguing with a customer about a price. Tim went up to one of the employees there and asked what time that guy got off, pointing towards Chris, because he didn't want to be here as long as he would have to deal with him. The employee told Tim he leaves around four thirty but we are open till eight if you would like to come back then. Tim thanked him for the info then turned and headed for the door turning off his phone.

Once Tim reached the car he opened the door getting in saying, "I hope you got all that because that man is a real pain in the ass, I don't see how his employees put up with him. If that was my boss I would have already knocked him out and quit on the first day.

Laughing I said to Tim "That is just the way he is and, yes I got every bit of that. Now we need to go shopping and get a safety vest, orange flag and some walkie talkies so that I can make this plan work. Oh and we need to find us a road barrier to borrow also if possible. It might not be today but if it all goes according to my plan it will be tomorrow and nobody will have to put up with him ever again." Pulling away from the curb I headed for a pawn shop to see if I could find some of the things we were going to need.

Finding a pawn shop near the edge of town I decided to stop in to look around and see what they had. When Tim and I entered a husky looking old man behind the counter asked what he could help us with. Telling him I was just looking to see if he might have some things that I was looking for, he told me that what ever was out on the floor was for sale and if I didn't see what I needed to ask him for it he might still have it. Looking around I found an old set of walkie talkies and noticed that he had some new safety vests behind the counter also some flags. Taking the walkie talkies up to the counter I ask if they still worked and also asked about the safety vests and flags. Picking up the devices he looked them over and popped the back cover off of them then replaced the batteries. Turning them on he handed one to Tim and told him to go outside, after Tim had went out side he started talking on the one he had and then I heard Tim talk back. Looking at me he told me that now I knew that they still worked but they were only good for about two miles. Now if I was to buy them and the vest for forty dollars he would throw in a flag for free. Happily handing him the cash I walked out with just about everything I needed. Now I needed to find some road construction where I could get one of their wooden barriers to take with me to use.

We went driving around town looking for some construction sites, so we could "borrow" one of their road barriers, discretely of course. But we were shit out of luck on that matter; there weren't many sites to begin with. Reluctantly we gave up, and decided to go back to our room so they could come up with an alternate option. On our back we just happened to find one on what appeared to be some farm property. The barrier was sitting at the end of the driveway, so I had Tim pull up closer and I jumped out and snatched it up before anybody noticed.

Knowing we couldn't go back to the room with it sticking out of the trunk, so I instructed Tim to pass the room with out stopping for the moment, so we could find somewhere to stash it out of sight, somewhere close to the tracks. Checking the time, I noticed we wouldn't have time today to follow through with what I had planned today, but tomorrow would be a different story. After hiding the barrier in a pile of brush close to the road but out of sight, we headed back to our room for the night.

Once we arrived at the motel, I began to run all of my plans by Tim, making sure he was up to speed. I gave Tim all of the details I had collected about Chris, including the car he drove. I told him whenever he noticed that Chris was coming, to grab the barrier and put it across the road, while standing behind it waving the flag we got for the occasion to signal him to stop, and be sure to have you're your vest on. After he stops, call me on the walkie talkie and let me know he's there. If he actually inquires as to what is going on, just tell him that there was a work site accident, and they were trying to clear it out as quickly as they could. I'll respond when I'm ready for you to let him through. Once he's through, dismantle the barrier and toss it in a ditch somewhere out of site, and leave your vest and flag there too. I will be by to pick you up shortly after you let him through then we will continue on to Billings tomorrow.

"Wait shouldn't we be leaving right after that?" Tim asked.

"No they will be too busy with the mess that will be there to know there was even a hit, it will all look like a tragic accident with one casualty. If they come by and evacuate the hotel, then we will continue on then." I told him.

"Damn, I can hardly wait to see what you have up your sleeve this time, since I have seen some of the things you have come up with." Tim said excitedly.

"That makes two of us, I am not sure how this is going to play out myself." I said.

With that being said we both started to laugh, but for now it was just time to relax and wait for tomorrow. Giving Tim some money I told him to take the charger and go and get us a couple of pizzas so we could have dinner, and I could check out my special gun in private. After Tim had left I locked the door and pulled the drapes closed. Opening the case with my laser rifle I began to inspect it and clean it for tomorrow, making sure that there would be no problem with it when I needed it tomorrow afternoon. I wasn't totally sure of what I was going to do yet, but I was sure something would come to mind when the time came. Just as I was putting up my rifle I heard Tim pull up. "Perfect timing," I thought to myself as I unlocked the door so he could bring dinner in. Once inside, Tim sat the food down and handed me my change, then we instantly began opening the boxes, while we started making small talk about a lot of little unimportant topics, as we ate to help pass the time.

At one point of the conversation, Tim began discussing his time while in the military. He mentioned that he spent four years total overseas before making the decision to walk away while he still could, via honorable discharge. He was curious so he asked why I myself never decided to join. In response I told him, "I did try, but my application to join was turned down. I passed all of their tactical training and ability testing, but failed my psych test with the white coats. They said that they couldn't use my type of mind set overseas so they declined my effort. I was also informed that due to the application that I had signed, and because of my attitude, that if they had of sent me, I would never have made it back home, if not physically, certainly not mentally. Those crazy sons of bitches were looking for people that didn't want to go, and that had no desire to utilize the required deadly weaponry needed."

"Damn, you were declared 4-F, what kind of contract were you trying to sign? What branch did you apply for?" Tim asked me.

"I was trying to get approved for a 30 year retirement contract, which allowed different options after five years. If it were up to me, I would spend my first five years with the USMC, after that I would go back again to basic training, so that I could become officially USMC-SF1. What that means, is that for the next 25 years, I'd be recruited and sent alone, on one way missions only." I explained.

"Oh, now it's starting to make sense. You were crazy back then too huh? You still haven't changed much! I really have no idea how my sister has been able to put up with you for this long!" Tim replied, with a shit eating grin on his face.

"You're not much better off mentally yourself, look who you hang out with even now." I said jokingly. At that, we both started laughing.

After they finished dinner, they turned the TV on and began searching for something entertaining to watch. While Tim was flipping through the channels, I decided to give Sara a call, just to check in on her, and see how she and the kids were doing. Talking to Sara on the phone, I caught up on the latest gossip around town. I informed Sara that Tim and I were on another job up in Billings but that we were still on the road and hadn't gotten there yet. At this moment we were in Steamboat Springs, Colorado, and we had run into Chris Gynas, and we intended on taking care of that problem while they had the chance. After we were done with all of the news updates, I talked with the kids for a bit, before their bedtime. After I was done talking with the kids, Sara came back on the phone once more, asking me how I was planning on taking care of the problem I had mentioned earlier. I told her I wasn't sure yet, but if everything worked out, she might get to hear about it on the news there also. With that we said our good-byes for the night and I told her that I would call again when we got to Billings. Noting the time, I told Tim that I was going to take a shower and shave while he enjoyed whatever it was that he had found to watch.

After finishing up in the bathroom I noticed that the program that Tim was watching was going off, and that the news was about to come on. Tim looked over at me and told me it was his turn, as he headed for the bathroom with towel in hand. As I sat on the bed watching the news, while I was still trying to figure out how I was going to carry out the job tomorrow. Oh well, I would sleep on it tonight and hopefully something would come to mind during my sleep. I didn't hear anything eventful that was going on that would affect my plans that I would have for tomorrow. Tim was finally coming out of the bathroom and we needed to get our rest for tomorrow, we had a big day ahead of us.

As I woke up, I noticed that Tim was already up and moving around so I decided to take advantage of this by sending him out for breakfast. By the time that I had gotten up and dressed Tim was returning with foods we could eat and go scout out a good position to set up for today's operation. After we finished eating it was time to go look around at where we was going to be at when Chris came through.

Arriving at the train tracks I noticed that there was no where to park out of sight, so I would have to hide my car somewhere behind us. Going back about three quarters of a mile, there was a little cove I could pull into and hide my car. This would affect my plans a little, but I could live with that. I would have to let Tim in on the change, though. After thinking about it, it occurred to me that this might be for the better, seeing as how I still wasn't sure what was going to happen definitively. After I finally picked out a place that I was content with as far as where the car was going to be hidden, I began to explain to Tim how the plans had changed.

First of all, the car would be right here beside him, so after he finished taking down the barrier, all he had to do was make his way back to the car and wait on me to get there. As for me, I would have to make my way back on foot from the tracks, through the woods.

Tim shook his head a little confused, and then asked, "Yeah I understand, but shouldn't I be a little closer to the tracks? Oh, and how will I know when you're on the way back to the car?"

"No, you don't need to be any closer. That might be too dangerous. As far as how you'll know I'm on my way back to the car, you will know I'm coming, trust me. There will be a clue, not sure how much of a clue, but you won't miss it. For right now, we might as well go and find something to do for a while, and then grab some lunch before we have to start setting things up, and getting ready." I told Tim with a sadistic grin.

Heading into town again, I noticed a local school was having some kind of a fund raising event, with the entire community invited to attend. I decided that would be as good as any thing else we could have come up with, in order to pass the time. After spending a couple of hours at the school event slowly walking around from one booth to another, just looking at all of the treats and projects they had to offer to raise the funds. Once we ran out of booths to admire, we decided that the timing was perfect to start looking for lunch. We found some greasy food stands, and ate right where we were, until our bellies were satisfied.

After arriving back at our selected location, we began getting ready for the big event, then got ready to hide the car out of sight as planned. After that, Tim went to put the barricade together while I made my way up to the tracks, where I decided to await the arrival of the train. Once I was settled in my spot, I radioed Tim, in order to notify him that I was ready, and to make sure he was ready as well.

Taking out my laser rifle, I powered it up, and then waited for the perfect opportunity to present itself to me. Looking up, I saw the track light turn red indicating that a train was on the way. At the same time, Tim called me on the radio to let me know that he had spotted Chris heading towards them too, and he was preparing to stop him. Perfect. Every thing was going just like I had planned, and now all I had to do, was wait for the target to show itself to me.

As the train approached, I noted that there were quite a few lumber cars being pulled, and they appeared to be loaded heavily. Great, I thought to myself. Now all I needed to do was cut the cables that held the load in place, and then once the train reached the curve, there would be a loss of cargo right on top of any car that was unfortunate enough to waiting at the crossing. As the engine of the train barreled passed me, Tim called on the radio to let me know that he had managed to successfully stop Chris, right there like they had planned. Calculating the speed of the train and the distance Chris had to drive in order to get to the crossing, I waited about thirty seconds for the train to reach the crossing, and then after that I told Tim to go ahead and let him through. I then waited for Tim to let me know that he was on his way. I wanted to make sure that Chris was at the crossing waiting for the train to pass by, as this was part of the plan. Finding a nicely loaded lumber car, I aimed and fired my laser rifle, cutting the straps that held the load secure, and then I packed up and fled. I wasn't sure what was going to happen next.

I was about halfway to my car, when I heard the crash of lumber being spilled all over the road. The next noise I heard was chilling, even hair rising. As I looked behind me, I noticed that several train cars were jumping track, and turning over. It's a good thing that I had left when I did, since some of the cars had landed where I was hiding. After seeing this, I knew that we would have to get out of there ASAP, because some of the tankers that were being pulled held ammonia and other chemicals, including some that were chloride tankers. I knew it wouldn't be long now before law enforcement would move in on the scene, evacuating everybody within a ten mile radius of the track. At that, I tucked my guns under my arm and took off, heading towards my car in a dead run. As I got close enough to the car, to be heard, I yelled at Tim to open the trunk and have the car started, so we could get the hell out of there quickly.

CHAPTER 7

As I got into the car, I told Tim not to spin out but to leave as fast as he possibly could, without leaving any marks behind. As we pulled back onto the pavement, Tim was asking me, what the hell happened back there, so I began telling him how I had cut the straps on one of the lumber cars, and when the train went around the corner, it dumped all the wood on to the road, causing the big bang.

What I didn't know, was that they are balance loaded. This means that when it lost its load from one side, it became unbalanced, causing it to turn over, which in turn, caused the train itself to derail. So, not only did the lumber land on Chris, so did half of the train cars. Obviously, this caused more damage than expected.

"We need to get packing, because there were chemicals on that train also, and I am still fully expecting the police to come around that corner any minute now, and evacuate the entire area, probably real soon." I told with him, concerned.

Arriving back at our room, Tim and I began to pack everything up, so we could leave on a moments notice. I made sure to leave my special guns in the trunk of the car. While we waited, we went ahead and turned on the news, and discovered that all of the channels were airing the same special report about the train derailment. The news was explaining that because of the train wreck, there was an ammonia sulfate, chloride and formaldehyde leakage, coming from some of the damaged cars, and that there were officials onsite, evacuating the local area that would be affected, demanding that they leave the area immediately. A few minutes after hearing this, the motel manager started knocking at our door, telling us that we had to leave because of the incident that is currently being disclosed on the news. He also offered to reimburse me my money I had paid for the nights that we didn't get to use, but holding my hand up, I told him to keep it, since he and his family might need it. Besides, it was only a couple of nights anyway. As he walked away he told me, "Just leave the key in the door, since there will be hazmat teams coming by later, to make sure that everyone is out."

Shutting the door, I informed Tim that we had just gotten the notice to leave, and that we should take advantage of this situation, and continue on to Billings. Nodding his head in agreement, Tim grabbed his bag, as I grabbed mine, and we both headed for the car, leaving the room key in the door, as promised.

Pulling out onto the road we saw more fire trucks and ambulances than we realized that this town even had. Hell yeah! Not only had I made a memorable experience for this town, I also had one to put down in my own book! The only other thing I had on my mind now, was that I was getting hungry and I didn't want to hang around this town any longer than I had to. So that meant that I had to make plans to stop somewhere in the next town along our route, so that we both could get something to eat, and I could reestablish my reservations in Billings. As I looked into my rearview mirror, I saw James. He was sitting in the back seat, giving me the thumbs up sign, and in my imagination, he was also smiling, but that was in my own head, it wasn't something I could actually see.

As I drove along the highway, I mentioned my plans to Tim, mentioning that we should stop and get some gas, and something to eat before we got completely through the next town. Looking around Tim replied, "Sounds like a good idea to me, this town is buzzing way too much for my comfort. By the way, how did you manage to cut the straps on a moving train that was going that fast without being on it? Does it have anything to do with those cases that you always carry around? I need to know, because I am going to have to explain this to Rudy, you know he demands details as to what happened and how things went down." Tim insisted.

Thinking about what Tim was asking, I simply told him "Tell Rudy that I managed to take care of my business here without raising suspicion, and that I was able to make it look like an accident. As to how it was done, you don't need to know, neither does Rudy. That is a trade secret that only I have the privilege of such knowledge. Also, stop worrying about what I have in my cases, it will only cause you trouble, and such knowledge just might cost you your life. Also you might want to call Rudy now, and let him in on this because I don't want this mentioned again outside of this car."

Nodding his head in agreement, Tim pulled out his cell phone and made his call to Rudy. While he talked to Rudy on the phone, I listened in, so that I would know exactly what he was telling him, making sure that the story was told accurately as it actually happened, and helping correct any mistakes that were made in the narration of events. Tim told the story just like I told him to, and finished up with telling Rudy that he would call him back once we arrived in Billings and got set up there. After hanging up the phone, Tim began telling me how Rudy was pleased with the fact that I was able to take care of my business so quickly, and discretely, and that we were already on our way to take care of the job in Billings. Then we began looking around for someplace for us to stop and gas up and eat before we continued on our way.

Finding a truck stop at the outside edge of the next town, we stopped and took care of our needs for food, gas and relieving ourselves. Pulling up to the pump, I handed Tim the money to go in and have them turn the pump on, and told him that I would meet him at the table in the café. Finishing up at the pump, I moved my car out of the way and then headed inside to get my change from the gas, and I found out that this town was effected just as much as the town we had left behind with the train wreck. From there I headed straight for the restroom, for a much needed relief. Afterwards I met up with Tim, and I informed him of the news that I had found out at the station register when I got my change. As I told Tim, he got a smirk on his face, and chuckled as he shook his head from side to side. Then looking at our menus, we made our choice for dinner and placed our orders, and then Tim excused himself for his own personal reasons. I decided to take this time to reinstate our reservation in Billings.

Unknown to me at that time, Tim also went to use this time to call Rudy back, giving him a lot more information about the train wreck then I had authorized him to give. By the time Tim had finished giving him all of the details that he could, Rudy was beginning to get real interested in those cases of mine that he was told about. Once Tim had finished talking with Rudy, and had used the time to relieve himself, he returned to the table. Right away, I noticed a change in his demeanor, and difference in his facial expression. I watched him for a few minutes, before asking him what was wrong.

Shaking his head, Tim simply responded, "You can't get away from them anywhere I swear, I was being hit on and asked out on a date by a guy in the bathroom. The worst part was he didn't want to take no for an answer. For a minute I thought he was going to follow me over here to the table!"

That had me laughing good, and I jokingly replied, "That's the consequences of looking so cute!" Then I laughed even harder, while he glared at me. Even though he gave me an acceptable excuse, in the back of my mind for some reason I knew that he wasn't telling me the whole story. I couldn't prove anything yet, but I decided it would be in my best interest to come up with a plan that would help me keep better track of him, and what he was up to when he wasn't in front of me. While we were still sitting there waiting for our food, I began searching on the internet through my phone for any undetectable spy ware that I could apply on his phone, without him noticing. That would give me a little better peace of mind if anything. I finally found one app that would let me record all of his phone calls, and follow his movements through GPS, as well as listen in to live conversations at my request. Perfect. Now all I had to do was get a hold of his phone without him noticing so I could download the spy ware. I sat there for a while pondering, then it occurred to me that I could get his phone and do what needed to be done once we got to Billings, and got ourselves settled in a room. I could take advantage while he was in the shower, and he would never know.

Once we finally got our food, we ate in silence, and then headed back to the car so we could continue on our way. With the good time we were making we should be in Billings in a matter of hours. With Tim behind the wheel now, I decided to close my eyes and take a quick cat nap, after making sure Tim knew where we were headed and the location of the hotel I had reserved.

After what seemed like a short amount of time, Tim was waking me up, letting me know that we were almost at our destination. As I became aware of my surroundings, I rubbed my eyes still a little out of it, and began paying attention to everything around me as we approached the hotel. Pulling into the parking lot, Tim pulled up in front of the office, and waited for me as I got out and went inside to claim our reservation. I retrieved our room key, and signed the receipt, and I was given the room number and told where to find the room. Thankfully it was on the bottom floor, being as how there were 4 stories in this hotel. Getting back into the car, I informed Tim of our room number, and informed him that the room was paid for and reserved for two weeks. But I also let him know that we could keep the room longer than that if the need arose, but I didn't think that would be necessary.

We pulled up in front of our room, and began retrieving our belongings and personal effects, and placing them inside. Once we were finished, I let Tim know he could go ahead and take his shower first, I was going to call the wife and kids to check in on them. He gathered his things he would need in the shower, and didn't waste any time heading for the bathroom in a hurry, after putting his phone on the charger, informing me he was glad we got there when we did, because he couldn't hold it any longer, and gratefully shut the door behind him. Unfortunately the walls were a little thin, so I grabbed his phone and walked outside to take care of business, giving him some much needed privacy.

I quickly downloaded the spy ware app on his phone, and then returned it to its place on the table by his bed, on the charger like I found it. While I had his phone though, I did notice the second call he made to Rudy, and the time and length of the call, realizing that he was making secret calls to Rudy, and not mentioning a word to me about it. Since it was still early, I decided to shout to Tim through the door that I was going to go for a walk, while I was talking to the family, and that I would be back soon. Grabbing the room key and my phone, I left the room, heading down the sidewalk that was there for that purpose. I was enjoying the sights, while I dialed Sara to check in and see how she and the kids were doing. She answered after the third ring, and I was grateful to hear her sweet voice as she greeted me enthusiastically. I could hear the kids playing in the back ground, and all seemed well as far as I could tell. We talked for a while, assuring each other that things were as they should be at the moment, and telling each other how much one missed the other, then I told the kids I loved them before we said our goodbyes, and ended the call. As I hung up the phone, I could feel an icy hand on my shoulder, and assuming it was James, I turned and looked around, but I didn't see anyone, or anything there, but after a few moments I heard her.

There was no mistaking that cackling voice, I knew immediately that it was the old witch. Then she spoke to me, telling me that we would be meeting again in 21 days, in Shreveport, Louisiana. She said she would inform me at another time, the exact place we would be meeting, and time. She told me that I needed to consider and think hard about any questions or information that I was seeking from her, so that I would be prepared when the time came, and she would answer my questions then. Then her voice faded away as usual, laughing as she always did with that creepy tone that was customary from her.

Well, that put things into perspective so to speak, now I had a time line I had to follow, and it was not a meeting I wanted to miss. Now I needed to start making plans from there, and figuring out what had to be done, and when, so that everything fell into place. Now I knew that I didn't have more than two weeks to complete our task here, because after that I had to head towards Louisiana. The governor now only had two weeks left to live, and didn't have any clue as to what was coming.

Returning to the room, Tim was already done with his shower, and sitting on his bed flipping through the channels of the TV, looking for anything interesting to watch. As I walked through the door entering the room, he looked up and asked me if I enjoyed my walk. I sat down on my own bed, across from Tim, and asked him if he remembered the old witch that I had told him about. He nodded his head, indicating that he did remember. I informed Tim that while I was on my walk, the old witch decided to visit me, and gave me some instructions that I had to follow. I also informed him that we had to be in Louisiana in 21 days, and that it was non-negotiable. That meant that we only had 14 days to complete this job, and that was it. I wanted to make sure he knew ahead of time, so that there would be no questions asked when the time came.

He seemed a little speechless for the moment, but he nodded his head in agreement. I don't think he even knew how to respond to that, even if he could. But you could tell by the look on his face that he took it seriously, and didn't even bother to try to question what he was just told. As I got up to gather the things I would need for my own shower, I told Tim that if he had any questions that he could think about it while I showered, and ask me when I was finished.

As I stood under the water in the shower, I thought to myself that one thing I could honestly say I was grateful for, was that the hot water never ran out at the hotels. As I enjoyed the hot water running down my back, I began plotting and thinking about how we were going to take care of this assignment. I didn't have much information or details about the task at hand, which meant that I would have to investigate and come up with my own information and possible options to complete my job. But I wasn't worried, I was getting used to it. It comes with the job.

After finishing up, I laid down on my bed, and looking up at the ceiling, I was going over the days events, and hoping that this job would prove to be simple and quick, so that we could get out of there without any hitches. Tim finally got over the shock of what I told him, and asked me, "Does this mean that you are finally going to get to ask the questions you have, and get some answers? That way you could share what this is all about to me and Sara?"

I thought about it for a moment, and then replied, "I hope so, I am tired of being in the dark myself. Let's go ahead and call it a night, we need to get some rest so that we can be at our best tomorrow."

As we woke up the next morning, we quickly headed out the door, grabbing coffee and a snack along the way. Using what information I did have, we tracked down Mr. Hemsley, and we followed him around for a while, gathering more information about him, and his whereabouts, so that we could start planning as soon as possible what method would we could use to do the job as effectively and quickly as possible. I was surprised that anyone of his level of importance would actually go to a cheap, unknown burger joint to get lunch such as this one. We followed him around all day, taking notes on his whereabouts and daily activities. As it began getting late, we decided that would be sufficient for the day, we would continue tomorrow, and then started heading back towards the room, so they could go over and compare notes. We ordered some drive through from a small diner that they had passed earlier this morning, so that they could grab some dinner along the way.

Once we got back to our room, we both sat down to eat before starting the process of comparing notes and deciding what information might be of use. After we finished going over the notes, we began our nightly routine of showering and getting ready for bed. We both fell asleep watching some horror movie on the TV that sucked. It was more comical to me than scary, so I simply lost interest and it didn't take long before I fell asleep, oblivious to the world.

Waking to the phone ringing that we had set up as an alarm, we got up and readied ourselves again for another long day of gathering more information. This is the process we followed everyday for the whole week, just to make sure we had enough information before we began plotting the job at hand.

Gathering up all the information that we had collected over the past week, Tim and I started to go over everything to see if we could see a pattern. After about an hour we discovered that after lunch every day Matt would go to the same place and spend over an hour there. This must be his side chicks' house since it wasn't his place, or where his wife and kids lived, which was typical for someone in power like him. Making plans I put on an old corduroy shirt and jeans, informing Tim that I was going out to check out a lead that I had noticed in our earlier observations.

Taking down the address that the governor always went to after lunch, I headed in that direction. Parking about a block away from where I was going, I grabbed a clipboard and placed what looked like a contract on it, and then started walking towards the house. Knocking on the door a very young looking, attractive woman wearing a very small bikini answered the door. Trying not to get caught staring at her, I told her that I was with a roofing company doing some work in the area, and was wondering if she would like for me to schedule a time for someone to come by and give her an evaluation of the condition of her roof at no charge. Shaking her head no, she informed me that her roof was only two years old, and that it wouldn't be necessary at this time, but thanked me for asking, and then she shut the door. Returning to my car I knew that I needed to figure out a way to get inside, and I was thinking to myself that it shouldn't be too difficult, I only wanted in so I could look around. As I got back into my car, I received a notification on my phone indicating that my spy ware was working, and that it had a new recording for me to review, from Tim's phone.

As I sat behind the steering wheel, I pulled up my app and tapped on the new notice from the phone, listening carefully as it played. "Tim this is Rudy, I have checked out the information that you gave me last week on the train wreck and I have something to tell you. After some investigating, they found that the wreck was caused by something that severed the straps on one of the lumber carts, and that as of yet they haven't been able to find anything that could have caused this disaster naturally, so now it is being classified as an intentional act of terrorism instead of an accident. Now what that means, is that the feds will also be getting involved with this investigation, which now makes it imperative that you figure out what Paul is hiding in those cases. If what he has is as deadly as you have been told, then we don't need or want the government getting a hold of these for certain." Then I heard Tim talking, "I know that but he has an elaborate locking system on them and he never lets me around him when he has them open so I haven't been able to see what he has in there yet. But don't you worry about it too much, I will figure out a way to find out what it is he is hiding. I can't do much about it right now because he is out, checking out the usefulness of some of the information that we have come up with over the last week, and still coming up with more useful information along the way, which appears to be a constant habit of his almost every where he goes. According to Paul we will be leaving here with the job done by the end of the week and heading towards Shreveport for some type of meeting he has set up that has to do with his past somehow. All I can tell you right now is that he has been acting awfully strange lately, and that this meeting is supposed to be able to explain whatever it is that has been bothering him and causing this strange behavior." Rudy simply replied, "Alright just keep me informed," and then at that they both just hung up.

Now I knew for sure that my suspicions were right and that I could never let Tim or anyone else find out what I had made, and the contents of my cases. I also knew now that I couldn't include him in any other plans that I would be making to do with this job either, because now I knew that I couldn't trust him anymore. After I was done listening, I pulled up closer to the house that I had just visited and left, so that I could keep an eye on it for now and take notes on the hour she decided to leave, that way I could get up there closer and have a better look around, so I waited and watched. After about half an hour, I noticed her pulling out of the driveway in her Bentley, and I decided to take advantage of the opportunity to go in and take a look around the house, and see what I could find out.

Creeping up to the house, I started looking around taking note of what I could learn about the set up of the house, and all of its surrounding property. Finding the gas meter, I peered into the window that was closest so that I could find out what room it was nearest. I just might need to use that to my advantage. Perfect, it was the bedroom. Now my plans began forming in my head, and I made sure to leave a camera there on the ledge before leaving, and then I checked all of my supplies to make sure that I had what I would need to carry out my plans, and also making sure to activate the camera I had left there intentionally before I left the house. Looking through my supplies I found everything that I would need to get the job here done, so that things would go so much easier and faster. It was time now for me to return to the room and find out what kind of story Tim had made up for what he had been doing while I was gone.

Calling Tim's phone, while on my way back to the room, I asked him if he has lunch taken care of, or if I needed to stop and grab something on the way to the room. He said he hadn't left the room himself yet, meaning he didn't have lunch, but he did have something to tell me when I got back.

I stopped at a quick burger café, and ordered us a couple of burgers, fries and drinks to go, then sat down and waited for my order to be called. This took about 8 minutes, and then I was on my way back to our room, lunch in tow. Once I arrived, I parked in my normal spot, and just sat there for a moment, thinking about what had to be done now that the circumstances had changed, and Tim could no longer be trusted. After a few minutes, I grabbed our lunch, and headed inside, greeting Tim as I walked into the room. I took everything from the bags, separating our meals, placing his in front of him, and arranging mine likewise.

As we began eating, I asked Tim what it was that he said he wanted to talk to me about. Looking over at me he replied, "Rudy called to check on everything, and see how we were doing. I told him that everything seemed to be going well, and that according to you, we should be done with this job by the weeks end. I also remembered to let him know that we would need a week off after the job was completed, to recoup, and take care of some personal business. He said that would be fine, no problem. He says just to make sure to submit all details and proof as usual before we take off, and to let him know when we got back and was ready for the next assignment. I told him that sounded great, and that we'd let him know when were back and ready for the next round."

Knowing that isn't exactly what was talked about I just nodded and continued eating. After finishing off my burger I informed Tim that I would be going out again tomorrow, that I didn't get all the information I needed today but I was confident that I would have all I needed tomorrow. Also I needed for him to continue to go over the information that we had already collected and see if he could find any similarities. Tim just nodded in agreement as he continued to eat. Now I had everything in order so I could get things set up to take care of the job myself with out any interruptions, or having to give explanations on what I was doing. I have already have my plans for the most part on what I was going to have to do, so now all I had to do was get back there and do it. Oh well, that would have to wait until tomorrow, but if things went as planned, we would be out of here in no time. Taking out my cell phone I pulled up the camera that I had left there at the house I was at earlier so I could see if there was anything of interest happening so far that was of interest or that might be useful. So far, I could see that Mr. Hemsley had made his routine stop, and that he was "hard at work" with the young girl from the house I visited earlier. I was going to have to revise my plans slightly, so I looked him up online, making sure that I have access to all of his friends and family, and any other contacts for him that I could find. Not only was I going to complete this mission, but I was going to drag his name though the mud as deeply as I could while I was at it. For right now though, I was going to enjoy what was left of today, and take care of the rest tomorrow.

CHAPTER 8

As the phone sounded its alarm the next morning, I sat up, and before I did anything else, I checked my phone to make sure that the camera I had left behind at the targets house was still functioning like it was supposed to. After verifying that all was good, I set the camera to the motion detection mode that would notify me every time it was activated by any movement. After seeing that all was well and working, I took care of my morning necessities, then began packing up my things and getting everything ready to go. By the time that I had finished, Tim was just starting to wake up also. I informed him that we would be leaving today, and advised him to go ahead and start packing so things would be ready to go when the time came. I informed him that while he was getting his things ready, that I had something to take care of and that I would be back in about an hour, seeing as how my things were already packed and waiting by the door. That being said, I left Tim to take care of his things, while I headed back to the targets house.

As I arrived, I made sure to park the car about a block away, to avoid being noticed. I got out of the car, and walked around to the back of the car and opened the trunk, so I could prepare a small duffle bag with the things that I would need to take with me to get the job done. Once I had everything I needed, I pulled up the camera app again, so I could see if there was any kind of movement or changes before I got there. I saw that the woman was still there in bed asleep, which meant that I would have to be extremely quiet and careful as I executed the plans I had, and

I reminded myself that I needed to be as quick as I could, before anyone noticed anything amiss.

I quietly made my way over to the gas meter, and setting my bag down there beside it, I opened it, removing a small charge that I had brought with me. I attached the appropriate wires to the proper places that would assure an explosion when activated correctly. That meant that not only would my devise leave a big impression, being as how I intentionally wired it to the house gas lines, it would make one hell of explosion, that would bring the entire house down, and then some. Once that part of the job was finished, I returned to the car, and headed to one of the local stores to purchase a disposable phone, and then I headed back to the motel.

Once I got back to my room, Tim looked up and asked me, "Are we already leaving, what about the job?" Without looking up I replied, "Don't worry, the job will be done before we leave. For now, let's get everything packed up and in the car. We still have a couple of hours before the fun begins." With a confused look on his face, Tim simply nodded and began getting everything squared away in the car.

Once we had cleared everything out of the room, we both got into the car, and I pulled around to the office and returned the room key before heading out. I headed towards a local sandwich shop, and we both went inside to get some much needed coffee, and a for breakfast sandwich. While I waiting for the notification from my phone that the motion detector had been activated. Finally, after an hour or more, I got the notification that I had been waiting for. As I reviewed the video feed that I was receiving, I pulled up Mr. Hemsley's contact list that I had, and began transmitting the live video feed to all of them, friends and family alike, which totaled around two or three thousand different contacts, including his wife. The funny thing was, the video was catching him red-handed in action while lying in bed with that same woman again. As the video was streaming, I pulled out the disposable phone I had just bought and tossed it over to Tim, with a number already pulled up, and told him to call the number on the screen. Catching the phone as it was tossed to him, he asked jokingly, "What's it going to do, explode?" as he pressed the call button. After the phone rang the second time, they both suddenly heard a loud exploding sound, that even shook the table slightly they were sitting at. After the explosion, I turned my attention back to my phone once more. Rewinding the video, I got to watch Mr. Hemsley blow up along with his girlfriend, and then the feed went blank. Forwarding the video to the disposable phone, I told Tim to watch it. And then I told him to forward it to Rudy, and then destroy the phone. Tim's eyes widened as he watched the video. He asked me when did that happen, and I replied, "Just now, you pulled the trigger so to speak with the call you just made. With a surprised look he pulled out his phone and looked up Rudy's number so he could forward the video.

Looking over at me Tim spoke up with "You are going to have to explain this to me so that I can give the details to Rudy when he calls back. Also I thought we were going to be doing this job together not like this, looks like I was on the outside and wasn't needed at all. It kind of makes me feel that I am not needed or that something is going on that I am not aware of."

"No there isn't anything going on, it's just that I saw an opportunity and took advantage of it. Don't worry I will fill you in on all the details you need so that you can pass them along to Rudy. Now finish up your meal and we will run by over there so that we can take some pictures with that phone before its destroyed." I told Tim.

Nodding in agreement Tim wolfed down the rest of his food and then got up to pay the tab and leave, while I followed behind him. Since Tim still didn't know where we were going, or how to get there, I got in the drivers seat so I could get us to the place we needed to be so he could take his pictures.

Arriving back at scene where Matt was killed at I parked as close as possible, then we both walked over to get the shots that was needed to send to Rudy. As we got closer we could see the emergency personal wheeling out the bodies and putting out the fire that had ignited from the explosion. Pulling out the phone I gave Tim, he started taking pictures immediately, and then after a few minutes Tim nudged me letting me know that he had collected enough to send and was ready to go.

Once we got back to the car, we climbed inside and sat there for a moment, and then I began giving Tim the details that I wanted him to forward to Rudy. Tim listened attentively while I gave him several very specific details. After I was done giving him what I wanted him to know, he forwarded the pictures he was told to send to Rudy, and then afterwards, he called Rudy to speak with him directly. He made sure to ask Rudy if he had received the pictures that were sent yet, and once confirmed he began recanting the details of the hit, in the order he was given, with as much detail as he could. Unknown to Tim, the conversation he was having with Rudy at this very moment was being recorded and routed to my cell phone, with more of the spy ware that I had collected for this exact purpose. Once Tim and Rudy had finished talking, they both hung up the phone on their own end, and then Tim turned to me and asked, "Now what's next?"

"Simple." I replied. "Now we are headed to Shreveport like we discussed, but let's get rid of that phone before we do anything else."

"Do you have any new information about this meeting yet?" Tim asked me.

"No, but I won't be getting anymore details until I get there, and I'm not really sure how, but I was promised it would be delivered on time," I answered.

"Good, maybe can finally get to the bottom of all this and figure out what is going on." Tim said with a serious expression.

At that, we headed to the nearest gas station so we could fill the gas tank, and perform a quick look over to make sure that everything was still in good working condition before heading out on yet another long journey. After getting gas and finishing with the check up on the car, I pulled up the map app on my phone so I could make sure that I had decided on the best route to get where we were going.

I still wasn't sure how I was going to handle the situation with Tim, but I was hoping that by the time this meeting we were heading towards now was over, I will have come up with something useful. For now, all I had to look forward to was the long drive ahead of us for the next several hours, and hearing Tim snore as he dozed off several times while it was my turn to drive.

As we drove along, I still couldn't help but wonder how I was supposed to make contact, or communicate that I was there, but I was sure that somehow "she" would know when and what to do next. I know she hasn't had any problems with finding me everywhere else I've been, so I had no reason to believe that this trip would be any different. Losing myself deep in all these restless thoughts, I kept my eyes focused on the road, while trying to make sense of everything in my head. The one thing I was hoping for is that my good buddy James would be present at this meeting as well. Oh well, I guess I'll just have to wait and see what happens. In the meantime, I would focus on the drive ahead of me, it was a 23 hour drive not including the necessary stops that we would have to make along the way for food and gas. I figured we could switch out drivers every couple hours when we stopped for gas.

I pulled up to a truck stop in Casper, Wyoming, we fueled the car up, and took the opportunity to get something to eat. There wasn't very many options here, so we settled for some home made burgers and fries. Looking over at Tim, I asked him if he felt like driving for a while, because he was looking kind of pale, like he wasn't feeling very good. Tim shook his head, mumbling something incoherent, and then continued to sit there quietly. I suggested that since we were a few days ahead of schedule, it might be a good idea to call it a day, and rent a room for the night, so he could get some rest, and hopefully be feeling better in the morning. Tim simply gestured a thumbs up, while he began picking through the food that had just been set before him on the table.

After our meal, I pulled into an Inn that was along side the freeway we were traveling, and got a room paid for the night. It didn't take much to convince Tim to get a shower and lay down for a while, he looked as though he was ready to collapse as it was.

Once he had showered and was lying on his bed, Tim spoke up asking, "How do you deal with all of the gruesomeness we saw today, like it was nothing? It didn't seem to bother you at all. At first, what I saw didn't bother me so much, but now it seems the more I think about it, the sicker I feel to my stomach. It amazes me that emergency responders of all kinds see this stuff on a daily basis and it doesn't seem to interrupt their lives either."

After thinking about it for a moment, I responded to Tim's question saying, "It is a skill you have to learn, to erase things like that out of your head. You might not ever forget it, but you don't think about it constantly either. You have to learn to control your emotions, and thought process, and train yourself to not feel anything at all, or you won't make it in this field of work. I do understand that seeing a body can be traumatizing, but when you've seen bodies that have been blown apart, it's even harder to deal with and process. And being as how that is what is bothering you, you should be feeling much better by morning." At that, Tim turned over on his side and in a short time was already asleep, oblivious to the world around him.

I decided to take advantage of the free time I had, and go for a walk. Pitifully, there wasn't much to see out here where we were, but I guess it was better than nothing. As I slowly walked along the way, I noticed something small blowing towards me, like a piece of trash or paper. As it got closer, I realized it was a twenty dollar bill, so I snatched it up out of mid air as it got close enough, smiling to myself. As I examined the bill, I noticed that on the front of it, there was something written on it. Ironically it read, "Glad to see you decided to come." Oh well, it caught me off guard there for a minute, but once I was over the initial shock, I shoved it into my pocket, thinking to myself regardless money was still money. Now I would have something to show off to Tim in the morning. After a few more minutes, I decided that I had had enough for the day, and I began making my way back to our room so I could try to get some rest as well.

As I slowly awoke the next morning, I turned towards Tim, and asked him if he was feeling any better today. He looked up at me, and then shaking his head, he headed towards the bathroom. Remembering the bill that I had found yesterday, I pulled it out of my pocket so I could show Tim, however, to my surprise the writing that had been there was gone completely. Irritated, I shoved it back into my pocket, deciding to just keep it to myself since I no longer had any way to prove it. Once Tim finally came out of the bathroom, I decided he looked a lot better, so I suggested that we both go get something to eat before we get back on the road again. Tim shook his head in response, saying that all he was interested in was some coffee this morning, nothing more. But he made sure to tell me that if I was hungry, to get something to eat for myself, regardless. Since Tim obviously still wasn't doing great, I decided it best for me to take first drive. After checking us out of the room, we made a quick stop at the nearest café, and after I grabbed a bite to eat we ordered two coffees to go, and then we were back out on the road again.

After listening to the radio for a little while, I told Tim that he could pick out a different station for a while if he wanted to. He declined, shaking his head no, and then leaned his head against the window, closing his eyes once more. Starting to wonder what was going on with Tim, I continued driving.

It was quickly becoming obvious that this line of work was not going to work out for Tim. As for me, the work doesn't bother me one bit at all. The thing that has me worried right now is this upcoming meeting in Louisiana. Was I even ready for what I was about to find out? And also, what was I going to do about what Tim had found out that he wasn't supposed to know, and what he was trying to do with that knowledge? All I could really hope for is that all would be answered and taken care of soon. Oh well, I would wake Tim up to see how he was doing at the next fill up. Maybe he would be up to driving for a bit then. In the mean time all I had to do was concentrate on getting there. If all goes like I have it planned, we should be there by sometime tonight.

After driving now for about four hours non stop, I was getting hungry, and the car was getting thirsty, so it was time for a stop. Reaching over and shaking Tim awake, I told him that we would be stopping soon and asked if he was feeling good enough to drive from here on for awhile.

Rubbing his eyes and yawning, he slowly began to wake up. He did look a lot better than what he had looked like earlier. As Tim looked over at me I could tell he was feeling better, especially after he told me that he was glad that we were stopping. He said he was finally starting to get hungry, and that he needed to find a restroom sometime soon as well.

Getting off the next exit we came upon, I headed towards the truck stop that was advertised all over the place on most of the local bill boards for the last several miles. It was one of the nicer looking truck stops that we had come across so far. Pulling up to one of the gas pumps, I got out to fill the car up, while Tim went inside to pay for the gas so they would go ahead and turn the pump on, and then went on to use the restroom. Once the car was full, I moved it to a parking spot on the other side in front of the café, and then went inside to meet up with Tim so we could order something to eat.

I suggested to Tim that he might consider ordering something light, being as how he has been sick for the last few days. While we waited on our order, I told Tim that since he was supposed to be driving from here, that if he felt sick again for whatever reason to let me know. I told him it would be better if he wasn't doing so well to just pull over and let me take it from there, with no hard feelings. He agreed, saying he was feeling better for now though. We ate our lunch in silence, a small meal, then took care of any other personal needs we might have before returning to the car, because we wouldn't be stopping again for another long while, at least not unless we had to.

On our way out of the door, I noticed an ambulance team pull up, on their lunch break, so I decided to take advantage of the situation. I asked one of them if they wouldn't mind taking Tim's temperature before heading out, just to be on the safe side. The team leader asked me why I thought it was necessary and I told them that he had been feeling sick the last few days, with nausea and loss of appetite. I figured since we are traveling a long distance, it would be safer to make sure that he was fit to drive, so I could rest easy while he had the wheel. The EMT agreed, saying it would be no problem, that in fact they could go ahead and do a complete vital check just to be on the safe side, and there would be no charge if that was all.

The EMT in charge told Tim to follow him around to the back of the ambulance, and to have a seat right there in the door frame, and to give him a few minutes to get everything together and hooked up. I stood right there beside the ambulance, simply watching them take his vitals, while making small talk with the driver. Once they were finished, I was told that his vitals were good. The only thing that did stand out, was that his blood pressure was slightly elevated, but it was nothing to be extremely concerned about. The EMT did agree with me about the driving however, and also told Tim that if he was feeling sick again or light headed or drowsy, to say something and relinquish the wheel, they would not advise him to continue driving while feeling sickly, or out of it. I thanked them for their time, and then we headed back to car, finally ready to get out of here.

Once we got back on the highway, after a few minutes Tim glanced over sideways at me and said, "Thanks. I wouldn't have thought of asking those guys. But I really do appreciate you looking out for me back there." Then he returned his focus back to the road.

I had my head leaning back against the chair with my eyes closed, and at his comment, without even opening my eyes I responded, "No problem. I knew they would probably be happy to do it, without causing a big ordeal. I had a friend years ago that was an EMT driver, and they would do that for anyone at any time, as long as that was all that was required. Anything more, and you would have to pay for it, but a vital check usually doesn't cost a thing." With that said, I leaned my seat a little further back, and laying in a more comfortable position, I simply began to doze off, while listening to the radio.

The next time I opened my eyes, it was because a change in the tempo of the car. I felt the car slowing down, so when I did fully become aware of my surroundings, I realized that Tim was pulling into another truck stop, and that the sun had already gone down. That meant that I had slept the whole time that Tim was driving. As I sat up, I looked over at Tim and asked him, "Where exactly are we right now?"

Tim looked over at me and responded, "We are about 100 miles yet from the Louisiana border. I have been driving now for almost four hours, so I figured now is a good time to stop and get gas and take care of a few things. Besides, I am really starting to get tired, so I figure it is your turn to drive now for a while."

"Sounds good to me, but you get to pump the gas this time, and I'll go pay," I told him, as I starting walking towards the entrance. After taking care of the gas bill and getting the pump turned on, I headed straight for the bathroom, grateful that there no wait to get inside. Once I had taken care of my needs, I stopped at one of the registers and ordered us some drinks and sandwiches to take on the road with us. I decided it would be best to eat on the go for now. Once we reach Shreveport, we could afford the time to stop and eat wherever we wanted to if we were still hungry, but for now we needed to keep moving. Before leaving I decided that I should go ahead and get a large coffee to go with that order, being as how it was my turn to drive. With my hands full of the food I had just ordered, I headed out to the car, passing Tim, who was on his way in to take of his own needs before we left.

I got settled in behind the wheel once more, waiting for Tim to get done with his business and get back so we get out of here, all the while I was thinking to myself that from where we are now, we should be in

Shreveport in our room in around three hours give or take. As soon as Tim made it back to the car, we headed once more; next stop, our hotel room in Shreveport. With that thought on my mind, I scuffed down my sandwich, and coffee, then turned my attention solely on getting to our destination. It didn't take long for Tim to finish his meal also, and within minutes after eating, he was already snoring softly, falling fast asleep, exhausted from driving earlier, and being as how he was still not feeling his best.

I began wondering to myself again, in what manner I was going to be contacted this time. The last time I was contacted it was that $20 that I found on the ground outside, with the special message just for me. Then I began smiling to myself, thinking maybe this time he would use a bigger bill. Or maybe even leave me an anonymous credit card laying around for my use only. At least the thought put a smile on my face. Checking the distance, I told myself only 2 more hours to go.

Time seemed to fly by at a rapid rate, as I continued down the highway. Before I knew it, we were passing the state sign that said in bright, giant letters, WELCOME TO LOUISIANA! That meant that we should be arriving in Shreveport within the next half hour or so. I started to wake Tim up, but then decided that it would best if I let him sleep until I had the room set up and ready to go before bothering him. To me, he still didn't look that great. As we crossed into Shreveport, I began looking for the nearest motel, and it didn't take long before finding a decent looking place to stop and get a room. After paying for the room and parking the car in front, I woke Tim up, letting him know that we had made it, and told him that there was a bed already waiting for him, he simply needed to help me unload the necessary items from the car, so that he could lie back down and go to sleep. He drowsily got up and gathered the toiletries I had handed him, and went inside leaving everything on my bed, and then walking over to his own bed and flopping down.

After getting all of my own stuff into the room, I decided to follow suit and get in bed myself since I was tired too from driving. Tomorrow would be another day and hopefully it would be a better one. As I lay there in bed trying to go to sleep, I began to wonder if this trip to Louisiana had anything to do with the way Tim was feeling, on top of everything else he was dealing with. Thinking back about it he didn't start getting sick until we were on the way here. It didn't seem like a very likely or logical explanation, but things here lately haven't made much sense or logic anyways, so it wasn't impossible. I guess we would find out soon enough, hopefully. Oh well, for right now, I needed to get some rest. There would be plenty of time to wonder about logistics tomorrow. Closing my eyes, I forced all thoughts from my mind, allowing myself to relax and fall asleep.

As I awoke the next morning, I felt a tingling go down my spine. I got up out of bed, and walked over to where Tim was still asleep, and placed my palm to his forehead, checking to see if he had a fever. I didn't notice anything out of the ordinary, he didn't seem feverish, so I was hoping that today he would be back to 100%. Even though he had betrayed me and lost my trust, he was still my brother in law, and I still needed him with me for now.

I still had no clue as to what the plan was, but for the moment, I was going to find some coffee and something to eat. Leaving the room I was off to find somewhere that I could get some food and drink for us both. As soon as I had gotten what I came for I returned to my room. Pulling up to my room I noticed an envelope taped to the door. Taking the food and coffee in, I snatched the letter off the door as I went inside. After setting the food down on a table, I looked the letter over and there was no name or any indication as to whom it was addressed to, so after waking Tim and telling him that breakfast was served, I opened the letter and began reading.

"Hi Paul,

Sorry I left before the job was done; it really wasn't my plan or choice. As you well know I have never left you alone on any of your adventures or problems and I never would. I am glad you chose to make it here in such a timely fashion though. The meeting that you have been looking for is being scheduled for tomorrow night at seven pm. Am sorry that it has taken so long before you have been set up with a meeting to explain what's being expected of you, but you still had a lot to learn first. Your brother-in-law is now sick because he can't handle any of the stuff going on around him, but he will recover with help. Also thanks for doing your best to carry out my last request, even though the fact is you were not allowed to do just like I wanted; you tried your best. I am still happy that it turned out the way it did. You will find a map on how to get to the meeting on the back of this letter, and be sure to bring your brother-in-law along, so that he can be cured. He will be in good enough health to accompany you. All your problems and questions will be answered there. See you soon, James"

It was hard for me to believe that I got a letter from James since he had been dead for almost a year now. Looking on the back I found a map that took us on a trip right into the middle of the swamp, where there was nothing but bugs, water and gators. Tim had finally gotten up and was sitting at the table drinking his coffee and eating, when I turned to him to inform him that he was now invited to the meeting and it was mandatory that he be there. Showing the map to Tim he just looked at it and nodded his head in confirmation. Grabbing my phone I decided to snap a picture of the map just in case it disappeared like the writing on the twenty dollars had.

After taking a sip of his coffee Tim spoke up saying, "I am glad that I have finally been included in this meeting so that I can ask a few questions that I want answered for myself."

"Yeah," I said. "Maybe I can get a bunch of questions I have answered, but I am sure that doesn't mean that I will like all of the answers that I will get." Oh well, the first thing I need to do is find out if Tim is feeling better, and from there we can find something to do to occupy our time until it's time to be at our destination, or you could say meeting point. After verifying that Tim was feeling much better today, we decided to go for a drive, checking out the local tourist sights, and simply enjoying ourselves for the day.

CHAPTER 9

While we were out, I decided to take advantage of being around the locals, and asked a few people here if they were familiar with the area I had indicated, or if they knew anything about where the place on my map was located, and how to get there. It wasn't until I came across an old timer, sitting on a bench with a cigar between his teeth, that I was able to get any kind of helpful information.

The old timer looked the map over for a few minutes, and then looked up and said, "Yup, I know right where this place is, but you couldn't pay me enough of anything to get me to go back there now, or ever again. You see, that area of the swamp is haunted. Many people have gone there, but only a very few have ever returned, and the ones that did somehow return have never been right in the head again. Legend has it that a very powerful witch lives there to this day, even though it is fabled that she was killed some hundred or so years ago. I advise you to take my advice and stay away from there young man. If it's fishing you are interested in, I can show you to a lot of places to go that are a lot safer. The biggest problem you are going to have trying to get to this swamp you are after, is finding someone willing to take you there. Anyone that knows the place will never set foot there because of the curse."

After a moments pause the old timer decided to give me his number, and as he turned to leave he said, "If you decide that you just want to go sight seeing or maybe do some fishing here locally, just let me know, I'm the right one to call, but don't even think about asking me to help you get to that place, because it's not going to happen."

Quickly grabbing his arm gently before he could leave, I asked him how far he would be willing to take us, and how much he would charge for doing so. All I would ask after that would be that he point us in the right direction before he leaves. The old man stood there for a few moments considering the offer, and then responded saying, "If you two are that dead set on going there, I guess I can take you as far as the trail that leads directly to the place you're after, for two hundred. Just remember I won't go in there with you, and I'm not about to wait for you to come back out either." I quickly agreed to the old mans terms, then we made plans on when, where, and what time we would meet up so we could be on our way.

Returning back over to where Tim was standing admiring a nearby pond, I informed him that I hade hired a guide to take us into the swamp so that we would not get lost. Tim looked relived when I mentioned that, so I didn't tell him the rest of what I had found out, about the fact that the guide would not be taking us all the way there. Tim would find that out on a need to know basis, like when it happened. With that thought in my head I silently laughed to myself while smiling.

With that taken care of Tim and I returned to our sight seeing of the city, simply wasting time until it was time to head back to our room and start getting ready. One thing I began to notice was that for the last few days, as the sun went down Tim looked like he was getting sick again. Oh well, I was told that this would be taken care of soon, hopefully tomorrow night. Right now all we had to do was get through tonight and we would face the other problems tomorrow.

After several hours of sight seeing, we returned back to our room, grabbing our dinner for the night that we had ordered on the way over so that it would be ready by the time we got there, and we could eat while we watched TV in our room. Tim admitted that he wasn't feeling his best, but he was doing good so we just sat there making small talk and laughing at the comedian on the TV until it was getting pretty late which meant that it was time to get some sleep.

As I awoke the next morning, my stomach was in knots. Today was the day I was finally going to get my answers, ready or not. Our up coming trip to the swamp was also on my mind. What would we be facing in there alone? How would we get back out? And most importantly, would we be mentally sane after getting back? These are questions that I wasn't about to share with Tim. I don't think he could handle more stress or anxiety at the present time. It was all I could do to keep my own composure I didn't need to have to put up with Tim's nervousness. Taking a page from when I was with James I decided to go find something relaxing to do, maybe find a duck pond and feed the ducks. That sounded like a good idea to me so that I could relive a lot of stress, and also take some stuff so that Tim and I could have something like a picnic until the time came for us to get to the meeting. Making the suggestion to Tim he said that it sounded like a good idea to him that it had been a long time since he had done anything like that.

Leaving our motel room we headed for a store where we could get the necessities for our little picnic in the park, making sure to get an extra loaf of bread to feed the ducks and birds with. After looking around for a while, we found the perfect little place. There were several mothers with their children, all running around and playing, and there was a small pond there, with ducks and geese swimming around. It was just what we needed. When we weren't feeding the ducks, we could sit back and watch the children playing, and running around, and simply enjoy the day. Tim was acting like he felt good today, laughing and playing with a few of the kids, and then feeding the ducks with their help. It made me start thinking of my own kids and Sara, as I watched the children here playing, so I decided to take the time to call Sara, and talk with my own kids, and see how they were doing.

While I was talking to Sara and the kids, Tim returned back to where I was, and asked if it would be alright to talk to his sister while I still had her on the phone, after I was done, before I hung up. I nodded my head, and then I handed him my phone, and decided to walk over to the edge of the pond and feed the ducks and geese with the extra bread I had brought along for that purpose. As I stood there watching them gobble up the treat I was tossing at them, and I started wondering if they ever had problems like I do, or anything similar to it, that would affect them like it does us.

As the day went on, the time came for us to leave, and go meet up with the old timer so we could get started on our journey to the swamp, where we were supposed to have our meeting. Signaling to Tim that it was time to go, we finished up what was left of our little picnic by tossing the leftovers of bread into the pond, which attracted all of the ducks and geese over to where it landed in the water, where they competed for the scraps. Then we headed to the parking lot where we had left the car parked, and loaded up, and pulled out of the park heading to our next destination.

Arriving at the place we were supposed to meet our guide, I noticed we were about ten minutes early, and the old timer had yet to show. I kind of wondered if he would even bother showing up or not, but then about five minutes later I noticed him pulling up. Seeing us already waiting there, he walked up to us and looked at me, asking if I remembered the terms he had set forth, and if I had the money to pay him. I simply responded with a positive nod of my head, and handed him his money. Taking the money, he pointed to an old boat down on the water, and at that we headed down to the boat, and we were on our way. The sun was starting to go down now, and the swamp started looking more and more spookier, as the sun got lower. After about forty-five minutes the old timer nudged the boat up to a trail that came down to the water, and handed us a flashlight. As we got out of the boat the old timer pushed off and pointed down the path we were standing on telling me that all we had to do was follow the path for about three miles, and we would be where we were trying to get to.

Shocked, Tim looked at me and said in high tone of voice, "What the hell is going on? I thought you said that you hired a guide to take us there. Now he just dumps off here in the middle of the swamp and leaves us here, and here you act like its no big deal? You could have at least left them two cases back in the car!"

Looking back at Tim I calmly said "This is as far as I could get anyone to bring us. What you don't know is that this part of the swamp is considered cursed, therefore no one will enter these parts. I didn't tell you because I was not going to put up with your whining and crying about it. Now as far as how we will get out, I'm pretty sure I will be provided with what I need to know when the meeting is over. Now we need to get going down that path or we will never get there in time, and we'll never get out of here either, so just suck it up buttercup, and get a move on." With that said, I turned towards the trail and I began my hike to the meeting and Tim did the same.

We had been on the trail for about thirty minutes when we came to a fork in the path. Wondering if we should take the left or right fork, Tim and I both looked up at the sudden sound of rustling in the leaves nearby. We both looked up in time to see a very large snake start to crawl across the left fork, so we both took that as a signal from the old witch telling us which way to go, and we were not about to get into it with a snake of that size. After traveling down the path for a while we noticed the outline of an old shack off in the distance in the fog that was rising. Apparently that was our destination, and we just had to get over there now. Looking at my watch, we still had about forty-five minutes before we were supposed to be there yet. Pressing on, we made our way towards the shack. The closer we got to it, the thicker the fog became, and not to mention the fact that there was spider webs everywhere. When we finally got there, I walked up to the door and knocked, and I heard the old witch answer in a loud voice, "Come on in." Tim and I entered at the witch's invitation, and looking around, we saw that there were spider webs everywhere inside the shack as well, along with quite a few snakes slithering around.

As Tim shut the door behind us, the old witch stepped into the room and introduced herself by saying, "Hello, my name is Marie Hubbard, and I'm glad you could make it, welcome to my place. I have lived out here in this swamp since the late sixteen hundreds.

You guys are a little early, not everyone has arrived yet, so have a seat, and make yourself at home. Oh, and don't mind the snakes you see here, they are friendly as long as you are invited. But as a warning, don't touch anything here without permission because it could be dangerous and/or life threatening. We are still waiting on two other guests to appear, so while we're waiting, let me take a look at your friend here, and see if I can find out what has been making him sick lately."

She gently grabbed Tim by the jawbone, and then looking Tim in the eyes, she pulled down on his cheek and then opening his eye even wider, she picked up his right hand and examined it. After she had finished looking Tim over, she laughed and simply said, "I can help him out, but it will have to wait until after we have finished our meeting. Oh my, my babies are telling me another one of our guests are arriving!"

I turned around towards the door as the indicated guest entered the room, and I was totally shocked when I saw that it was Detective Brown that had just entered. A few seconds later I could feel that all too familiar ice cold chill in the air, which meant only one thing. James was here.

I turned, looking around towards the front of the room, and I saw that I was exactly right. There, right before my very eyes stood the Grim Reaper himself in person. Now there were a total of five of us that had gathered here for the meeting, and from what I understood, we were all here now.

The old witch escorted Detective Brown up to the front of the room, and began to introduce everyone. "Ok everyone, this is Detective John Brown, and to my left here is James Crum, the Reaper. Here in the center of the room we have Paul Greer, with his sickly brother-in-law Timothy Mendoza, who will be needing my help later on. Now that we are all here, we can get this meeting started. First of all, Mr. Mendoza here is suffering from spiritual displacement. This comes from constantly being around someone that is surrounded by magical and spiritual forces like our friend Paul here. Now as for you Paul, you have many questions that you want answered because you don't understand what's going on with you. Well first off, we have this meeting every fifty years. James here has attended six of these meetings before you came around, and was just as confused as you on his first meeting. This one will be the hardest of all of them for you, since this meeting is your first. Detective Brown here is on his fourth meeting, but certainly not his last. We will try and get all your questions answered in order to help you with the transition into this job. Both Detective Brown and James were both in their twenties when they attended their first meeting, now look at them."

The witch continued by saying, "Now James, you will be able to speak for this meeting, so if you have anything you want to say, you can and should do so. Detective Brown will be around anytime you have any questions that you can't figure out for yourself after this meeting. James here will always be around to guide you when need it, so just remember that you will never be alone at any time. Now, I will give the floor to anyone else that has something to say."

At that point James began speaking saying, "I am sorry that I couldn't tell you everything that the job entailed, but that is against the rules for any new recruit to know all the details. Now you know how I had all that money saved up, I wasn't in this business for forty years, it was more like three hundred and forty years. John here has helped me change my identity a few times throughout the years before you showed up. He practically knows everything that I know, even about the weapons that you carry around in those cases. But he is not your enemy, he is your ally. He has been awfully busy here lately, covering up where you have been using those guns, so that higher up government officials won't be involved or interested in looking for them."

"Now before you ask YES, Sara and your kids will be long gone before you will. Someone with your ability and talent only comes along about every forth to sixth generation. You can't die until you find another person with the same potential abilities, and train them to take over for you. Then and only then, you get to replace me at this job, while I finally get to retire awhile before getting ready for the next round." James said definitively.

After James had finished speaking, Detective Brown took his turn, saying, "I have followed James around for a long time helping him out whenever he needed me. Now that it's your turn, I will give you my contact information so that you can reach me as needed."

Detective Brown continued, "The guns you created are great, but they are much too far advanced for our day and time and today's society. I have managed to cover up your use of them so far, but my suggestion to you is, put them away. Keep them out of sight and out of mind until a later date. My predecessor had to make the same suggestion to James about the gun that he had made. Now his gun is common knowledge, and sold everywhere. If you would like, you can leave them here with Maria, and she will take care of them until the time comes for them to be reintroduced to society. Maybe by our next meeting technology would have advanced enough so that you can have them out again without drawing any unnecessary attention."

"Now as for Sara and the kids go, we can take care of the last two targets on the hit list so that the contracts on them are voided, but as you know, if you stay around them long enough, more contracts will follow. I'm sorry to have to tell you this, but you know the only way to keep them safe is to stay away from them, and not be around them anymore after we take care of the last of this hit list." Detective Brown said reluctantly.

Continuing he said, "From here on, you will age one year for every twenty years that pass, which means that we have a long road ahead of us."

"Now, I know where John Mitchison and Pamela Garcia are currently located, as well as to where they are about to be going. Marie can take care of both of them together, and that will take care of your list, and since there will be no more payday, the contracts will be voided." With that said, Detective Brown continued, "Now it's your turn Paul, to ask whatever questions you might have."

Paul stood there for a moment then started speaking, "A lot of my questions have already been answered by some of what's been said already, but I do still have more. First of all, who am I working for, and how long will this last? And then will I ever be able to safely have a family of my own? And how exactly is Marie supposed to be taking care of the two that I am hunting? Are Tim and I going to be able to get out of this swamp without any complications, and will Tim be able to remember any of this? And then most importantly, what am I supposed to tell Sara about the sudden life changing situation. How do I tell her that I have to walk out of their lives permanently, and with no questions asked?

Marie stepped forward and said, "I'll answer these questions for you. Who you work for now is the universe, but I'll have to explain that one a little later. How long it will be has yet to be determined. It varies from person to person. We had one that worked with us for over six hundred years. And no, you never will be able to have a family of your own that will last for the same amount of time as you. And as for how I am going to take care of the two idiots you are looking for well, that is for me to know, but you can be a part of it and help if you want. As far as Tim goes, after the meeting you both will be escorted out of here, and he won't remember a thing, but neither will his boss. You will be a free agent again so to speak. We are doing this as a courtesy to you, like a welcoming gift so to speak. As far as Sara is concerned, you won't have to tell her anything. For all she will know, you came into the swamp and never returned. Now, do you have any more questions? Marie asked him while looking him straight in the eye.

Paul spoke up by saying, "Thank you, I would like to be a part of taking care of them though, I feel like that is my responsibility. They are my family whether they can see me or not. I don't feel right about the thought of simply walking out on them and abandoning them. Will Sara have access to both of our bank accounts?" Paul asked. "What if she looks for me and finds out I am somewhere else? Or how I be able to give her financial support, if I am supposedly not around to see it through?"

James looked up and said, "Now it's my turn. She will have the smaller account, but no memory of the other larger account that will continue to be at your disposal. Once we all leave here and go home, you will be receiving a new identity, and your residence will now be the condo you already own in Texas, and she will inherit the other property you currently have that is in West Texas. Also, all of your current information and identification will legally declare you deceased. Your new identification, birth certificate, and any and all other documents for your new identity that you will require, will already be prepared and waiting for you when you get to your condo. You will need to dispose of all other current documents and identifying papers that pertain to your current ID. You will also need to burn any mail that have your name on it, and make sure that the word gets out to any and all billing companies and collection agencies that you are deceased. Before you leave here, if you haven't already drawn up a legal will, you will need to do so, so that it can be taken care of right away." James finished.

Feeling a bit overwhelmed, I asked Marie when exactly we were going to be taking care of the two targets of mine, and when the situation with Tim was going to be taken care of. Marie replied saying, "We will take care of Tim now, and get him out of here. Since he won't be able to remember any of this, we will place him back home in his sister's house, so that when he wakes up in the morning, he will never know he left. As far as Sara is concerned, she will not remember anything from the last 48 hours, so she will have it in her head that he came home from work and has been there every since." Marie said with an amused look on her face.

"As for the two we are hunting, you will have to spend a few days here with me, so that we can get things straightened out and get everything done right."

CHAPTER 10

After Marie finished talking, she started gathering up a bunch of miscellaneous items, and then walked over to where Tim was standing and began mixing them up. Looking over her shoulder, Marie turned towards the rest of us saying, "You three need to wait outside until I call for you."

Obediently we all went outside closing the door behind us, meanwhile simply making small talk as we waited to be called back in. After about thirty minutes, the door opened again and Marie poked her head outside, motioning for us to come back inside. We entered single file, and as I looked over at Tim, he appeared to be in what looked like a catatonic state, almost as if he were zombified. Marie approached Detective Brown, and then handing him a crystal, she instructed him to place it one hand, while keeping his other hand firmly on Tim's shoulder. She reminded him all the while to make sure to keep his grip on the crystal tightly. She then instructed him to keep his grip on Tim's shoulder until they got to his sister's house. Once there, he was to remove his hand, while leaving Tim there asleep in his bed, as if nothing had ever happened. After leaving Tim there asleep, he was to squeeze the crystal one more time, in order to return. This would be a form of instant transportation, she had informed him. Once that was done, Detective Brown would return back here again with the rest of us, right where he should be.

Nodding his head in acknowledgment, Detective Brown did as he was instructed, and then he and Tim faded away right before our very eyes. I assumed that it would take a while before he got back, but to my surprise, he was right back where he was standing only minutes before, looking at all of us calmly. He then turned and looked at me, with a big smile on his face as he said simply, "She appears to be doing just fine, and so do the kids. Oh, and by the way, that is a beautiful home you have from what I could see. Now, let's see what needs to be done in order to help Marie take care of this problem of yours."

That said, Detective Brown then turned to towards Marie, and the two of them walked a short distance away, so that they could talk amongst themselves. I could hear them discussing something, but the hushed tones were too quiet to make out what they were saying, which obviously was the point.

As Detective Brown and Marie continued their discussion, James approached me, saying he wanted to talk with me a bit as well. As he stood next to me, he began his own conversation while looking me in the eyes.

"Paul, as I've mentioned to you before, I'm sorry that I couldn't tell you everything that was going on, and what all was involved, but I did try and give you a way out of this life. I also tried to give you a few clues as to what exactly you were about to get yourself into. But as soon as you showed me those guns you designed, I knew right away that this was going to be your rightful place, and that you were going to be the one to take my place. I just wish that I could have had more time, so that I could have trained you better and taught you more than I had the chance to."

Hanging my head down low, I responded to James saying, "Yeah, I know you warned me several different times, and that I refused to give it up, but I am aware that I brought most of this on myself. I don't blame you, or anyone else but myself. I know that I am the one that decided to design this new and better weapon. I simply didn't consider the consequences of how potentially dangerous they would be for everyone once discovered. In a way, I wish that I had never actually followed through with making all the different weapons that I made. Then I would still have my family, not standing here now looking at a life that no one would have wished for. Now I know what you meant, when you said that this was going to be a very lonely life. I already miss my family so much, but I know that they will be safe for now, and that is the one comfort that I have at the present moment. I guess I will have to be content with the simple knowledge at least that they are going to be OK. You know the funny thing is, I always said that I would protect them and even die for them, or whatever was necessary to assure their happiness and safety above my own in this lifetime. I just didn't realize how accurate that was going to turn out. And now as far as they know, I did die in order to save them. At least as far as their reality is concerned."

As I looked up at James, I had to wipe away a few tears of regret that were streaming down my face. Placing a hand on my shoulder, James said, "I am all too familiar with the regrets and how much it hurts, especially at first when all of this is still new. I've been there, and when I think about it, it still hurts to this day, almost as much as it did then. It is something that you will have to learn to live with for as long as you still walk this earth. Now don't get me wrong, you will never get over it, but you will learn how to live with it. There are always some actions and decisions in this life that you can never take back or erase, no matter how much you wish you could."

After they had finished talking, Marie called James over to where she and Detective Brown were still standing, and invited him to join in on the conversation they were having.

Simply standing right where I was, I was thinking to myself that I too would be called over soon to join them, and after about five minutes or so had passed, James turned towards me and motioned for me to come on over and join them.

Walking towards them, I began wondering what the conversation was going to be about this time, and once I made it over to where they were all gathered, Detective Brown looked at me directly, asking me if I knew anything about working on aircrafts. Looking back at him, I informed him that I understood the fundamentals and technical science behind them, but I had never actually worked on them myself. As Detective Brown stood there for a few moments thinking to himself, he finally asked me if I would be interested and willing to learn how to do the actual manual work on said aircraft, and if I was a quick learner. In response, I asked him how long of a time period were we discussing that I would be allowed to learn what was needed. His answer was that I would have seventy-two hours. Shaking my head no, I told him that it would be impossible to learn that much, in such a short time.

"Damn, I guess that rules out that idea," Detective Brown responded. "We will just have to come up with something else as far as that is concerned. In the meantime, I guess I will teach you as much as I can, with the time that we have. It might come in handy some day if you ever happen to need that kind of knowledge any time in the future, for whatever the reason may be. I would also like to teach you some better skills on how to be a little more discreet. I have seen your face in a few videos that you shouldn't have appeared in, and I have had to go in and delete them. But I guess for right now we can just focus on the problem at hand, which is getting rid of the last two targets on our list. And then we can finally have the contracts on your family removed indefinitely," he informed Paul.

"Thanks, I can use all the knowledge that I can get, being as how James didn't have enough time to teach me everything he wanted, and I needed to know." I responded.

"Now, I know that I'm on my own as far as learning anything and everything else I can, from anyone that is willing to teach me and educate me with whatever tools I will need, so that I can advance and become more familiar with my work. Before tonight, it never would have occurred to me to ask you for any type of help or assistance at all. As a matter of fact, I had been thinking it was going to be quite the opposite. I have always sort of thought of you as the enemy, someone that was here to stop me by any means possible," I informed Detective Brown.

After the conversation was over, Marie turned and walked over to a table that was located on the other side of the room, where she had a bunch of potions and strange colored powders arranged.

James then turned towards the two of us that still remained standing there and stated, "This is one of the reasons that we have these meetings every fifty years, so that we can update each other on what's been going on, and teach each other anything new that needs to be passed down, while catching up on each others news that we need or want to share with each other, that way we can keep doing what we do. Each one of us has different skills, and a different type of lifestyle that teaches us unique things, which in turn is useful concerning everyone, while sharing their own stories, opinions, and experiences, as well as new and useful methods that are presently being used around them, as well as in their own lives that could potentially be helpful to each other. Now, if it is an extremely urgent situation that cannot wait, the meeting can be called in at whatever time is actually required, but thankfully that hasn't happened as of yet, at least not in my time. As for the present being, Detective Brown is going teach you everything he can with what time that he has. Anything that does not get covered today will just have to be taken care of on a later date. In the meantime, after today's meeting just make sure you get some rest. Later, we will make the arrangements needed to meet with you at some other place and time, so he can finish teaching you what he can then. Oh, and by the way, he is also the one that can keep you updated on how your family is getting along, so that you can keep up with how they are doing, and know that they are still safe and doing well," James assured me.

"That sounds good to me, I could actually use someone to talk to from time to time, and by the sound of it, things are about to get pretty damn lonely," I told him, already picturing in my head how hard things were about to get. "The job is not the problem. The problem is being forced to leave my family behind, without even getting the chance to tell them goodbye or explain things. And it's not only my family, but my friends and everyone else that I have known my whole life, and all those who have had a hand in helping me along this road that we all call life. You know, sometimes life just sucks. Oh, and before I forget, just how long do these meetings typically last, because as you well know, I am on a time schedule now?" I asked James.

James responded saying, "Marie can make time stand still for up to seventy-two hours, which means that she can pause time, even if only for a couple of days. But after the seventy-two hours are up, time resumes back to normal right where it left off, like nothing ever happened. That is why you were told you only had seventy-two hours to learn everything you could about the mechanics and such for working on aircraft. But don't you worry yourself about it too much. You are extremely intelligent, and Detective Brown is highly skilled as well as being an excellent teacher. I have faith that you will learn a lot more than you could possibly expect by the time all of this is over."

"If you say so," I responded. "I'm not sure how much really, but I have been learning a lot as of lately. Several things that I had never even really considered, or would have believed for that matter, so I will certainly keep an open mind." Then I turned my gaze looking directly at Detective Brown and asked him, "When are we supposed to begin all of this training?"

Detective Brown held up his index finger, indicating for me to wait a moment, and then he turned around and walked over towards where Marie was standing. After saying a few words to her in hushed tones, Marie responded to him by simply nodding her head in confirmation. A few minutes later, she handed something over to him, and he held out his palm, accepting whatever it was that she had for him. After that, he turned back around towards me, and walked over to where I still remained standing, pointing towards the front door indicating that it was time to go.

As we both exited the door, Detective Brown gestured with his hand, indicating that I look over towards where he was pointing. As I turned and looked, there before me was a large clearing that didn't seem to be as foggy as everywhere else around here seemed. We made our way over to the clearing, and then with a wave of his hand, a hologram of a private jet appeared before us. We both approached the image, and Detective Brown began pointing out all of the different parts, naming them as he went. Hydraulics, elevators, ailerons, and rudders and so on. He then explained to me how each part functioned, and how it was designed to work, and what it was designed to do.

I was amazed at how easily and quickly I was catching on, and how it all was actually making sense in my mind. I truly didn't expect to catch on this quickly! And the most amazing part to me was the hydraulic pump. Without it, you might as well have ripped out its beating heart, because it couldn't function without it!

After he was through going over most of the exterior parts, he began showing me all of the controls inside the cockpit, and explaining to me in detail how each one of the controls and gages functioned. He reminded me several times how extremely important it was that I got all of this memorized, ASAP! He was however extremely talented with describing the details of how each and everything worked, so much so, that I was almost convinced I was actually ready to start flying right now! I could certainly visualize it for sure, in any case.

Next, he walked me over to the jet turbines, and went on to explain to me how the fuel lines worked, where they went in, where they came out, and all the functions in between. He then continued on to explain how everything functioned together, to actually get the plane off of the ground and into the air.

After he had finished, he waved his hand again like he had before, but this time the plane actually disappeared. Next, a giant flat movie screen appeared. Using this, he began to play multiple videos of myself, pointing out to me several errors that I had made lately, and literally pointing out to me multiple videos where I had appeared as the main character, that I never should have been caught on any recording, much less on video. As he continued on, he pointed out the multitude of hidden cameras that had been strategically placed all over the place, going unnoticed by the public for the most part, and then began teaching me how to recognize and avoid them in the future. As it had turned out, learning how to avoid being seen, was a lot harder than learning how to fly a plane. I was truly stunned by how many cameras were hidden all over the city. I learned quickly that you couldn't do anything or go anywhere, without big brother looking over your shoulder and watching you all the time. I also learned that the larger the town, the more cameras there were to avoid, and the more difficult they were to find. I was definitely convinced now that it was easier to learn how to fly a plane, than it was to avoid having your every move watched by somebody all the time.

While time may be standing still for everyone else, for me time was still moving on and I was starting to get hungry, and tired. I mentioned this to Detective Brown, and he nodded his head, replying that he too was beginning to get a little hungry himself, then asking me what sounded good to me. Jokingly, I told him that a burger and some fries with a cold drink would be great, but I don't see any of that out here. Smiling, Detective Brown replied that it sounded good to him too, and then he waved his hand over all of the images we had been studying, and they vanished back into the fog that they had appeared from.

Telling me to wait where I was, he went back inside, and as the door closed behind him I began to realize exactly where we were, and I began to wonder how long I would have lasted out here by myself, if not for the protection of Marie. After what only seemed a few moments, Detective Brown reappeared carrying two bags, as well as two drinks. As he handed me my share, I began to wonder if time stood still for me as well, while he was gone just now. I considered asking, but began eating my food instead. Then I began to wonder silently, all of the benefits that came with having the ability to make time stand still, such as how much could you get away with, as far as having to pay for the things acquired while time stood still, or was that even possible? I didn't doubt it, but I wasn't about to ask. I did ask however think to ask him how it was that he knew that I loved chocolate milkshakes, just like the one he had brought me with my meal he had just provided. He simply responded by saying, "Who doesn't?"

After we finished our meal, he waved his hand again at the fog, as he had done earlier, and the giant flat screen reappeared once more. This time, he began to show me some of the techniques that James used personally to avoid being seen or recorded. While Detective Brown was rambling on, my mind was elsewhere. I couldn't help but wonder what James and Maria were doing right now, or what plans they were hatching, so I could begin my part in all of this. I was distracted by my mixed emotions of both fear and excitement. I was ready to get this new chapter of my life started, but I knew better than to think that things were about to get any easier for me, it was just the thrill of a new beginning.

CHAPTER 11

As Detective Brown finally up today's lesson, he began going over what he had been teaching me, and asking me questions to test my level of understanding and knowledge of the lesson. He even questioned me about the mechanics of the aircraft lesson he had taught earlier. He seemed satisfied and even a little impressed by my fast learning ability and comprehension of the material being taught to me. He complimented me on my quick understanding and ability to keep up with everything, even though it was an overwhelming amount of information I was having to learn at an overwhelmingly rapid pace.

Detective Brown asked me if I wouldn't mind waiting outside a bit while he went inside to discuss today's progress and events with Marie and James. I told him that would be fine, but I wouldn't be going very far, I was more than a little concerned by some of the wildlife around here. Detective Brown shook his head amused, and informed me that I would be just fine, as long as I didn't wonder off too far by myself. At that, he walked inside, leaving me to my thoughts and doubts.

After what seemed like half an hour or so, James appeared in the doorway, motioning for me to join them inside. As I got to the door, James held the door for me to enter, informing me as I walked through the door that I was about be tested on everything that I had been taught so far. This time however, it would be with everyone present so that they could all judge for themselves my skill levels. Once inside, we all sat down around a rickety old wooden table, with the exception of Detective

Brown. He chose to stay on his feet, pacing back and forth as he mentally prepared himself for this round of questioning and testing.

While Detective Brown was mentally preparing himself for the questions he was going to ask James and Maria look at each other and smiled. Seeing her crack a smile would send a chill down your spine it was so frightening. When she turned and looked straight at me there was a grin on her face as she began to speak in her crackling old voice. "So Paul, do you think that you may have learned enough to help out with the original plan that we had thought up before you got here?" Maria inquired.

I thought about her question, considering everything I had recently learned as well, and answered hesitantly, "I'm not entirely sure, but I believe so. I guess we will find out soon enough. The test I'm about to take should answer that and more." The old woman nodded her head in agreement, and then we all continued to make small talk for the moment, waiting for Detective Brown to indicate that it was time for me to begin the testing that we had all been anxiously waiting for, especially me.

Finally Detective Brown raised a hand with his index finger pointed upwards, indicating that he was ready to begin administering the test we had been waiting on. "Question one", he began. "What is the most important functioning part on an aircraft?"

Thinking for a moment, I answered confidently, "That would be the hydraulic pump, it is the only system that has a working backup in the case of power failure or any other emergency. It is also the main part that allows the plane to turn, climb altitude, or descend in order to land."

Detective Brown nodded silently, and continued, "Question two. If you were to disable one of the engines, would that be sufficient to bring the aircraft down in a crash?"

Without hesitation, I answered. "No, they could continue on to the nearest landing space in the case of needed emergency landing, with the one engine for a short time."

He responded by giving me a thumbs up, indicating that I had answered correctly once again. "Question three." Is the aileron or the elevators more important on the plane?" The Detective asked.

After a moments thought, I responded the ailerons are more important, because you have to be able to turn left or right to line up to the runway, but you can always decelerate in order to come down. Detective Brown again nodded his head in approval, giving me another thumbs up for answering correctly. As Detective Brown continued asking me questions, regarding the different components and their locations, and I continued to answer all of his questions correctly, impressing everyone that was present during this test.

After 20 or so more questions, Maria interrupted with her cackling voice saying, I think I've heard enough. "Apparently he has done his research well, and has learned all subjects intended. She then turned to the detective saying, I must congratulate you as well. Because of your teaching skills, he has been able to learn quickly and understand all of the lessons that you have taught him." "Now moving forward, it is time to start making plans so we can put all of this education to use, Maria announced. She then stood up and walked towards the center of the room, over to the table that still held several of the magic potions and crystals that only she used or touched. At that, James stood up as well, following behind her. Then Detective Brown also fell in line behind the others, motioning for me to follow as well.

After we had all gathered up around Maria, she began to speak. "Now that we have what we need to complete this mission, we will go over the entire plan together." As she went over all of the material, I made sure to pay close attention so that I would not miss anything. I was beginning to feel like a school kid again with all the information that was being gone over. I knew how important it was to have all the facts straight, but there was a lot of information and subjects to be learned, and no paper or pencils to take notes. It was going to have to be committed to memory and become an automatic response. As she finished going over everything, Maria looked over at me and asked "Paul do you feel confident enough to carry out this mission without any questions or hesitations?"

Looking in her eyes I simply replied, "I will have no problem doing my part but I do have one request that I would like to ask you. Will there be any way that I can appear before them both, just for a few seconds, so that I can get their attention and laugh in their faces as they both realize that their time is over, and I won in the end?"

Maria simply laughed at my request, and then replied, "That manner of thinking is pure evil, but I do believe that I can accommodate your request but with one condition. When you appear, you must be accompanied by James when you appear before them. James will be along for the ride all the way to the ground just so he can make sure that the job is done right."

Worriedly, I thought for a moment and then asked, "Will there be any danger to James if he is on the plane when it hits the ground?"

James spoke up and responded to my question, "No, there will not be any problems since I am a spirit only when I am in that realm of reality. You can't kill or hurt the dead, you just have to put up with what they do, or the insane noises they make until they figure out how to move on for themselves. The only exception to that rule is that now you are stuck with me until the day comes that it is time to change the guard again and, that will be some time from now."

Smiling at James I just said "I am relieved to hear that, but as far as us being stuck together for an eternity, that is something I would think sounds a lot easier to deal with."

With that said, Maria broke in saying "I suggest we bring this meeting to an end for today. We can regroup in the morning around 9am if that sounds good for everyone." We all nodded in agreement, and then Maria began handing out crystals to each one of us, explaining that the crystals were only useful for two trips. Our first trip would get us out of here and this horrible swamp. The second one would get us all back here in morning so we can regroup and start our mission. Once I was handed my own, I turned to her and asked her how exactly they worked. She responded "Imagine in your mind where your car is sitting right now, then close your eyes and hold the crystal tightly in the palm of your hand. When you open your eyes you will be there. To get back again, do the same thing, but have the image of where you are right now in your mind. It is as simple as that."

After she finished explaining everything, I watched intently as both James and Detective Brown faded away right before my eyes. Hoping desperately that what she said was true, with no gimmicks, I too held my crystal tightly, and squeezing my eyes closed I did as I was told, and I too faded into nothingness for a few moments, reappearing right where she said I would.

After I reappeared next to my car, I placed the crystal in my pants pocket, and opening my eyes and looking around, my watch indicated that only 2-3 minutes had passed in time since I had left this exact place hours before for my meeting. Walking over to the muddy edges of the swamp, I was standing in the same place I had stood only a short while ago, before leading Tim to the old witches' habitat. As I looked across the muddy water, I could see the same old man that had led us to our destination with Maria, returning as well across the swamp, coming from the same direction that he had left to get us to our destination. Truth be told, this was a whole new experience for me. I was amazed by the traveling methods used by the old witch, being as how I had never believed in actual witches or witchcraft until now. One thing that I can say for sure though is that I was not interested in having to answer any questions, so I took that as a good sign to leave. I got into my car, and slowly drove away, returning to my motel room.

The day was still early, despite the time I spent in the swamp with my new team despite the lack of time lapse while I was away. Once entering my room, the last two days of events still on my mind, I fell on my bed and fell asleep from exhaustion.

When I opened my eyes I looked outside through the window of my room, noticing it had gotten dark already, so I checked my watch. It was three thirty in the morning, so reaching into my pocket I pulled out the crystal that had been given to me by the old witch. A jolt of unrealistic reality swept over me, with the realization that all of this was real, and not some fever, or fantasy for that matter, or anything else like it. It did mean however, that I had a meeting to attend in just a few hours. Well, it would be of no use to try and lay back down now. I would probably oversleep, and that I couldn't risk that happening. I might as well go get some breakfast and coffee. There's no telling when I would get the chance to eat again, especially during the meeting or the upcoming mission.

Arriving at a restaurant that was close by, and actually open at these hours, I was deep in thought as to everything that had been happening recently, breaking concentration only long enough to order food and drink. This is not what I had expected or wanted when I signed on for this business, but now it's gone too far to turn back. The only option now is to move forward from here. I still have to protect the family that I used to call my own, and keep them from any danger that comes their way, and this is the only way it can be done from now on. I now have to live in a world that exists only in most people's imagination, with no way out. It is a blessing, because I can do something to help my family out of danger. But it is a curse as well though, that in being able to do so, I have lost them forever.

After finishing breakfast I returned to my room, determined to get this done. I reached into my pocket grabbing the crystal I was given, trying to decide, whether or not I should go ahead and return, so that I could just get this over with. Looking at the time, it was only seven o'clock and wondered if I returned too early, if I would still be under Maria's protection, or if would I be on my own. I finally made the decision to wait, since I didn't want to chance it, so I sat down to watch a little bit of TV instead, until it was time to go.

While watching TV the thoughts of James began to fill my head, and I began wondering how many families he actually had. I had already met the one that was living right now. I know he mentioned how much it had hurt to lose his first family, but he never said how many families came after that, or if the one that I had met was indeed his first wife, and if she might have the same curse on her that we have.

This type of thinking sure takes up a lot of time and attention though, since when I actually looked and noticed the time, it was already now eight thirty, and I had no idea what had been playing on the TV that I was supposedly watching this whole time.

I stood up, heading towards the restroom to take care of my own personal business, then I made my way to the center of the room, and reaching into my pocket, I grabbed a hold of the crystal. I then closed my eyes, picturing the shack in the middle of the swamp where we were before, and hoping for the best as I squeezed the crystal tightly. Being slightly afraid to open my eyes, I still cracked one eye open slightly, and lo and behold I was back in the swamp, right where I had left from yesterday! Maria was emerging from the back room, and smiled at me when she saw me standing there, and so she motioned for me to sit down. Not long after my arrival, James appeared, followed by Detective Brown. Now all were present that were needed in order to carry out this mission.

Maria came forward and said, "Now that were all here, we'll go over what each person is required to do, one last time just be sure." "We have to be ready because the time they take off is ten fifteen, which means approximately thirty minutes after take-off, we must execute this plan."

I held a finger up, to catch everyone's attention, so I could direct a question at Maria, and once all eyes were on me, I asked Maria "Will we be able to hold our own, considering the amount of wind flow outside of the plane?"

Laughing with her usual crackling voice, Maria simply replied "There will be no wind flow, because I will have time temporarily standing still." "Also, you will not be there physically, only in ghost form, until you decide to appear in that last moment just so you can laugh in their faces. I will make sure time is moving then, just for that last minute. Now, does everyone know exactly what to do, and when?" Maria asked. Everyone nodded in affirmation, including myself. Continuing on, Maria then said "We still have a little bit of time before the scheduled take-off so, is anybody hungry?" Grinning widely, she offered a tray of what was supposed to be edible, but not only did it smell horrible, it looked just as bad, and actually appeared to be moving! She began her cackling laughter, at the look on everyone's faces, then set the tray down within reach, shrugging as she walked away.

With a look of utter disgust, Detective brown sat his own briefcase down on the table before us, revealing a dozen doughnuts. You could actually see the relief on everyone's faces!

A short time later Maria returned, and after a few moments she stepped to the center of the room, waving her hands as Detective Brown had done earlier, and again a large screen appeared before everyone. But the scenario was not the same. This time a small private jet-liner appeared, and looked to be awaiting it's passengers to finish boarding so they could take off on their scheduled flight. Maria spoke up then saying "We must pay close attention, in case they leave late or too soon. Now, this is the jet plane that both Pamela and John are going to be traveling in. If anything changes ahead of time, let me know immediately. Once they are airborne, the mission begins, and all of our duties become effective, which means no turning back!"

After that being said, she crossed over back to the other side of the room, where she had all her strange potions and such laid out. She picked out two bowls from the table, and began placing different ingredients in each one. After she had accumulated all the different ingredients she was after, she began walking towards Detective Brown and me, a bowl in each hand. She then placed one of each in front of both myself and the Detective, saying "You're probably not going to like this, but it is a necessary part of the procedure." Then she suddenly reached out, grabbing first my hand, then the detective's, pricking both of our fingers with a needle. She then squeezed a single drop of blood from each of us, into the bowls she had set before us. After that was done, she told us to mix the ingredients of each bowl by sloshing them gently around, and when the smoke began to arise from the bowls, they were instructed to inhale the vapor that was now rising. James had no need for this procedure, because he was already dead from this world, and he could this part on his own. Besides, she mentioned this was only for their protection.

I noticed that once I had inhaled all of the vapor, the scenario began to change. I looked up noticing that suddenly I was looking directly at both John and Pamela, right there in front of me. It gave me the sudden urge to start this mission right now, but I knew that I had to wait for the correct timing or I would ruin everything. But it wouldn't be too much longer now since they were already boarding, and would soon be airborne.

We all watched intently, waiting as the jet took off down the runway, and then jetted upwards, becoming airborne. We could hear the pilots communicating with the towers, announcing their climbing ascent into the air, aiming for thirty thousand feet to begin their journey. It took all of about five minutes to reach its goal, and then Maria announced, "Time to begin. First, Detective Brown will go and do his part and when he returns it will be your turn Paul, to do your part and scare them to death so to speak." Handing him a special crystal made just for this job, he nodded and gripped the stone, and then promptly vanished. We all watched Detective Brown do his job, and we watched as he pushed the elevators in a down fashion so that the plane would head straight for the ground, then he went under the plane and did something else, but the body of the plane hid what he was doing from the rest of us. I would guess that his time was up though, because he started to become transparent again to the point that he completely disappeared. A few seconds later he reappeared again, right beside me where he was when we began. Now, it was my turn. I gripped my crystal, and poof I was beside the plane! Poking my head through the skin of the plane I saw my target, the auxiliary hydraulic pump. Since time was paused the gears that ran it were standing still, but I also saw a bonus. The main fuel line that feeds both engines were right beside it. First, I looked over where the main hydraulic pump was supposed to be, but noticed that Detective Brown had done his job, so it was gone. All I had to do now, was place my hand on them both at the same time, and that would move them both with me, as I then appeared in the passenger compartment. I would then drop them on the floor right in front of John, and enjoy the look of sheer terror on his face when he realizes he is about to die, and that the Reaper is already standing right there behind me, waiting to take him and Pamela on their final trip.

I felt much like a school kid again, about to get away with something I knew I wasn't supposed to do. I almost couldn't wait until I was able to see it in reality, with my own eyes not just imagining what it was going to look like. It would be the image that would stay with me for all eternity, and would certainly help me get through this. Holding onto my targets, I waited to be pulled up into the interior of the plane. It didn't take long before a boney hand reached down and grabbed my shoulder, and I was on my way up!

As I got up to the level where James was, I looked back and there was John, accompanied by Pamela, who was sitting in his lap. This was going to be great! Walking over to where they were, I leaned over so that my face was between both of their faces. Reaching backwards, I gave a thumbs up to James, signaling that I was ready. James reached over and put a crystal in my hand, then he stood up and it was on. The first one to react was John, as his eyes widened and his mouth fell open.

Pamela started screaming and began squirming relentlessly to get out of Johns lap. They were both sure surprised to see me appear before them, especially at thirty thousand feet off the ground. After the initial shock wore off John asked, "How did you get on this plane, and where did you come from, and what do you want?"

"How did I get on this ride, I'm not really sure myself, but I know you're the reason I'm here. As to where I came from, search the darkest regions of you're mind. Now picture if you will, something so much worse, that even the darkest part of your mind is terrified, that's where I'm from. As for your last question, I am here to remove the payday and threat that you are responsible for placing on my family. And while we're here, let me introduce you to my friend, the Reaper!" I smiled, answering each question clearly, so that I was satisfied that he understood what was happening. "Oh, by the way, GAME OVER! I win!" And then tossed the parts I had removed off of his plane right at his feet, grinning like the devil. Satisfied, I again clutched the crystal tightly that James had given me, disappearing right before their eyes. Leaving John and Pamela to their own fate with the Reaper, who was right at their side all the way down.

As I reappeared at Maria's place, Detective Brown asked me if I had gotten any satisfaction off the mission. Nodding, and then smiling from ear to ear, became the only responses that I needed to hear.

The only question I had now, was how long it would be before we were able to see James again? But my curiosity was soon answered, as James appeared right before us. Shaking his head from side to side he pointed at me and said, "You are one sick bastard. Even Satan himself wouldn't have thought of doing what you did back there," James bragged!

Maria broke in with "Now that we have all the small stuff out of the way we need to focus on the important stuff like we need a new identity for Paul he cant keep using his old one since he is now known as dead. Detective Brown that is your field of expertise to take care of. We are counting on you and I know you can do it. Paul I have a little something for you to have and keep with you at all time. I think we have a good team now so I am looking forward to the next five hundred years if mankind makes it that long. With that Maria handed me a crystal and told me that it was my personal gem and anytime I felt I needed to I could use it to get to our meetings or just to talk to each other. This was my permanent stone for only my use. And as long as I keep it safe it will do the same for me. As far as the weapons you made they will probably be out in the next fifty to hundred years then I could have them back to use then and not raise any suspicions. Till then they would be kept in suspended animation so as not to degrade or rot. Detective Brown will bring you new ID to your apartment in Dallas. At that Detective Brown brought out four drinks and made sure each one of us had one and told me to grab my stone and think of where my car was because after this the meeting was over. We then clank our glasses together and as we took a drink from it everything faded and I appeared by my car and the news was talking about the plane crash that had just happened minutes ago killing all that was aboard. Thinking of the look of sheer terror and surprise that was on Johns face made me smile once more. The only thing left now was to check out and head for home and wait for the next mission and my new ID. It was a long drive back to Dallas and a little lonely since I had gotten used to having Tim with me everywhere I went, now all I have is James the Reaper for my constant companion. Now I know what James meant when he said that this was going to be a long and lonely life.

As I arrived at my condo in Dallas I entered through the door and began looking around thinking that this was all I have now so it was up to me to make the best of it. I thought about going down to the café to eat wondering if Alice would even remember me. Then thinking about it I needed to wait on my new ID in the mail before doing too much running around so that just in case someone asked me who I was I could answer without making it harder on Detective Brown. I went to lay down for awhile so I could rest a little while.

I was awakened by a knocking on my door getting up and answering the door I was surprised to see Detective Brown and James standing there. Detective Brown had a tan envelope he handed me telling me my new ID was in it and how glad he was that we would be working together for the next five hundred years according to Maria. He also informed me that they would always see me the same but no one else would see me as the man I once was before. He left me his number to get a hold of him if I needed to then turned and left. James entered and went over to the couch and sat down I made my way over and sat beside him just saying that now it was going to be us together from now on. Hearing this, we both just hung our heads down in unison, awaiting our next job or mission, whichever comes first!

SYNOPSIS

As Paul's life continued on, his friend James Crum (the Reaper) followed him every where he went, as Paul tries to make a name for himself. While he was out trying to make a name for himself, he also had to focus on getting the contracts that had been placed on his wife and kids heads removed, even if that meant that he had to die to save them. While he was trying to get the contracts removed, he had to work with his brother-in-law Tim, and as the time goes by, he finds out dark secrets that he wished he had never learned. Even though Paul did manage to save his family, he was forced to face an ugly truth, one that he wouldn't have wished on his worst enemy. Join along as Paul travels across the states in an action packed thriller of corruption, betrayal, witch craft and anguish as the old world meets the new world. As you begin finding out the real truth behind it all, ask yourself if this can really be happening behind the scenes, and if could it possibly be happening in your hometown too?!